Praise for *The Disintegrations*

"Has the feeling of a conversation between new friends, exploring the idea of death through several stories. . . . *The Disintegrations* is an unusual work of fiction that makes for a compelling reading experience."
The Gay and Lesbian Review

"Cobbles together nightmares, legends, haunts, and tender recall into a larger story that allows for deep reflection and interpretation. . . . McCartney presents briefly penned inquiries, snooping for small answers to the big question: What does the exploration of death reveal about life?"
Lunch Ticket

"A novel that reads like a journal—with all entries meditations on the theme of death."
Kirkus Reviews

"A book that takes possession of you right from the opening and will not let you go. Challenging and gripping, a rumination on death and memory that speaks eloquently to our sense of loss, both personal and communal. The writing is exquisite. In the best possible sense, I know this book will haunt me for the longest time."
Christos Tsiolkas, author of *Barracuda*

"Engrossing and reverent, *The Disintegrations* strangles death. A philosophy of the concrete and a reckoning of the ethereal, this novel dreams of all that has become lost in a world of remainders. We who remain may not find relief, but it leaves us dazzled and astonished and brutally satisfied with a gratitude for living."
Lily Hoang, author of *A Bestiary*

The Disintegrations

A Novel

Alistair McCartney

The University of Wisconsin Press

The University of Wisconsin Press
1930 Monroe Street, 3rd Floor
Madison, Wisconsin 53711-2059
uwpress.wisc.edu

Gray's Inn House, 127 Clerkenwell Road
London EC1R 5DB, United Kingdom
eurospanbookstore.com

Printed in the United States of America

This book may be available in a digital edition.

Library of Congress Cataloging-in-Publication Data

Names: McCartney, Alistair, author.
Title: The disintegrations: a novel / Alistair McCartney.
Description: Madison, Wisconsin: The University of Wisconsin Press, [2017]
Identifiers: LCCN 2017010426 | ISBN 9780299314705 (cloth: alk. paper)
Classification: LCC PS3613.C3565 D57 2017 | DDC 813/.6—dc23
LC record available at https://lccn.loc.gov/2017010426

ISBN 9780299314743 (pbk.: alk. paper)

For

the dead

who find themselves interred in this book.

And the dead were judged by what was written in the books, by what they had done.

Revelation 20:12

This is a novel, a product of the author's imagination. Even when real names of individuals or places are used, the characters, settings, and situations should not be mistaken for nonfiction; as someone once told me, *Death makes fiction of us all.*

Contents

The Disintegrations

The Weight

I know nothing about death. Absolutely nothing.

Do you want to know something?

I'm almost forty and I don't know anyone who has died.

Okay, sure, there was my Auntie Joan; she had these soft bones that just kind of crumbled. Then there was this kid Danny who went to my school. He dropped out, to take up a trade. Went up North to be an electrician and got tangled in some live wires.

And there are those people I read about in the newspaper, whom I almost feel I know, like that boy from UCLA who left his dorm at 3:00 a.m. The police dog followed the boy's scent to a bus stop where the trail ended and the scent disappeared. They found his skeleton a couple of years later in a basement in Oregon.

So I have known or known of some people but no one really close to me. That's a little weird, right?

As a result, I can't help thinking I'm deficient in something. I can't help . . . feeling I lack a certain, I don't know, a certain weight.

Holy Cross Cemetery

Let's see if I can come to grips with this.

When I'm at work, if I'm looking for death, I don't have to look very far. There's a cemetery across the street from the university where I teach.

Opened in 1927 by the Roman Catholic Archdiocese of Los Angeles, Holy Cross Cemetery covers approximately three hundred acres of land in Culver City.

There's a photo on the Internet of the inaugural ceremony. In the image, which is grainy, a lady wearing a hat with a veil concealing her face is in the process of cutting a black ribbon spanning the entrance gate, declaring the cemetery open for business. The crowd appears to be enjoying themselves. We can assume that many of them are still there; the Archdiocese was selling plots dirt cheap.

As far as cemeteries go, it's not much to look at. The headstones are all flat in the ground, I'm not sure why, something to do with space I suppose, or a symbolic function of which I'm unaware, and the trees are few and far between, so viewed from a distance, or without my glasses, it could almost be a golf course. Even the white marble box of the mausoleum on top of the hill could be mistaken for a golf clubhouse designed in the Brutalist fashion by some third-rate Le Corbusier.

Still, these three hundred–odd acres of consecrated ground serve as a point of orientation for me in my endeavors and for visitors to the university, which is located in one of five identical glass buildings and can be difficult to find.

4

Just look for the big metal cross on top of the cemetery gates, our receptionist says in response to the frequent inquiry: *Where are you? Where are we?*

My Grandma's Resurrection

*Someone more knowledgeable once told me: "When you
describe the dead, you should choose your words carefully."*

So I barely knew my grandma, but she frightened me. She bought a
special dress to die in, then she died on Easter Sunday, or thereabouts.
The timing of her death was . . . interesting. I'll return to that.

My memory of her is brittle, so let me get through this quickly.

My gran was my dad's mom, the last of my grandparents. Both my grand-
dads were gone before I was born—heart attack, brain hemorrhage—
and my mom's mother died when I was too young to remember.

Margaret McCartney lived in Motherwell, Scotland, this industrial
town just outside of Glasgow, known for its Catholics and its iron- and
steelworks.

It's a weird name, *Motherwell*, sort of witchy. There used to be a well
in the town, centuries ago, a holy site devoted to the Virgin Mary. The
well was filled in and covered up, but a plaque identified the site, not
too far from my gran's house, on Ladywell Road.

Apparently, when Dad immigrated to Australia, Gran refused to say
good-bye. But she stayed in touch. Once a week she would pop down
to the post office and send her son a pale-blue airmail letter.

If I happened to get the mail the day her letter arrived, I would read
the return address written in her intricate, lacy handwriting, her cursive
so tangled as to be almost illegible, and whisper the name to myself,

Motherwell, Motherwell, until the words blurred and lost their meaning—
or gained new meaning. I imagined there was still a well in that town, full
not of water but of mothers, who were trapped down there at the mossy
bottom.

Gran came to visit us twice. The distance between Glasgow Airport
and the airport for Perth, the capital of Western Australia and the place
where I was born, is 9,156 miles, a fact I memorized once and have never
forgotten. That's a long and arduous trip for an old lady.

My memory of her is so dry and brittle, she's almost disintegrating.

Let me try to describe her, because that's what we do: we offer physical
descriptions of people before they become skeletons, which are even
harder to characterize. Margaret McCartney, maiden name Queen, a
necessary modification of the name *Quinn,* was short and had gray curly
hair and wore wire-rimmed spectacles. She wore the same kind of dress
every day: dark blue, plain, like a nun's habit. When I asked her why,
she said *because it was practical.* If she spilled ink on her dress, *the stain
wouldn't show.*

I don't want to speak ill of the dead—I'm superstitious, you should
know that about me, it rules everything I do—but I don't recall her
being an especially warm person. She spent a good deal of time in her
room. She carried a Bible around our house and would read passages
aloud, but at a low, murmurous volume, so you couldn't hear the words,
marking the place with her finger. She was dour and she seemed to
bring the damp air of Scotland with her, so distinct from the dry heat of
Australia, like the damp rising from the bottom of a deep well, so deep
it could be bottomless.

Sometimes Gran would put down her Bible and talk of bad omens,
death omens, like she really was a witch: *Dogs howling for no apparent
reason, red specks appearing on linen, broken clocks that suddenly start*

ticking, three horses with the same coat standing together, cracks in freshly baked bread, a ringing in the ears and a knock on the door, which you open but nobody's there . . .

There were plenty more, but those are the ones I remember. I guess I learned something from Gran: anything could be sinister, dire, if you chanced upon it at the right moment.

This woman whom my father presumably came from seemed very . . . foreign, not just because of her accent, which chopped up her speech, so that everything she said was splintered, but because of her age.

You know how when you're a kid, there's something suspicious about old people, their skin, the way they smell, and you can't put your finger on why?

I think it comes down to this: all old people are foreign, because they're closer to death. That's what's disquieting about them. That explains the odor. Children have this vague floaty memory of the womb and its shadowy customs, but the elderly are on familiar terms with the customs of death, which are even shadier.

Though I was so young when Gran visited, I scarcely had a sense of her. Her handwriting was more vivid and real to me than her physical presence. It was as if I had never met her. Except there was a photo of us, overexposed, standing in the backyard, holding hands in front of the hibiscus bush. So we must have met.

Then one morning, and not just any morning, but Easter Sunday, I was in the kitchen, eating breakfast, when my mother came in. Still dressed in her cotton nightie, she told me she had *some sad news*: "Your gran has passed away."

I asked what Gran died of and Mom responded, "She died of old age. What a day to die," she muttered. "Easter, of all days."

I sat at the kitchen table and puzzled over my gran's death, like she or it was a mathematical problem, something abstract.

Of course, I have no idea how I felt when my mother relayed the news. I have to reconstruct every memory and every feeling, just to access the past.

I was aware of the solemnity of the occasion. Death required certain behavior, a specific tone of voice.

I must have been seven or eight and somehow I already knew this.

I was also alert to the mystery. Gran's death was like the Bermuda Triangle, all those planes that fell off the radar throughout the 1970s, vanishing without a trace. You don't hear about the Bermuda Triangle anymore; those planes must have stopped disappearing.

Or it was like the *Mary Celeste*, the ship that was sailing from New York to Italy in the nineteenth century; one month after leaving port, the ship was found floating in the Atlantic, abandoned. There was no sign of the crew members, the captain, or his wife and child. There was no evidence of any struggle. Nothing was out of place: the china and silverware were set; teacups held tea that was lukewarm; and there was something simmering on the stove.

Most of all, her death felt . . . far away. For all I knew, time differences aside, my gran was puttering around in the red brick council house my mother had described to me, reading aloud from the Gospel of Matthew or Mark or Luke or John, preparing to celebrate the Resurrection of Jesus, on the third day after his crucifixion.

As I sat there in the kitchen, trying to take it all in, sort it all out, I overheard Mom talking on the phone.

"They found her body on the floor in her bedroom, but they're not sure how long she had been dead. It could have been a day or two. They had to air the house, open all the windows. Isn't that dreadful?"

So my gran died sometime *between* Good Friday and Easter Sunday. Sometime between the first nail was hammered through the wrist of Jesus Christ, into the wood of the cross, and the moment he slithered out of the tomb, to show up for his unearthly resurrection.

That morning, the atmosphere in our house changed. My father did a lot of shouting when I was growing up—he could not contain his feelings—but the house got real quiet. My three brothers and my three sisters observed this silence. The dog stopped barking.

When Dad emerged from my parents' bedroom, I told him I was sorry about Gran and he was matter of fact.

"Well, these things happen," he said.

We all went to Mass in our Sunday best and it was hot. My dad had a few quiet words with the priest, who patted his arm. At the lectern, the priest sweated beneath his black robe and spoke of Easter and my grandmother.

"There was no better day of the year to die," he said.

He spoke of disintegration and resurrection.

I sat on the hard pew and listened to that story for the thousandth time; I had heard it so often it had been virtually drained of its enigmatic qualities, but I still waited for my favorite part, where Jesus asks Thomas to put his finger in the hole in his side.

The priest promised that my grandma would also return from the dead.

My dad sweated and wept.

After Mass, eager to get home to my Easter eggs before they were ruined by the warm weather, I looked for Gran in the sky, which I suppose was blue, but I could not see her.

There were several explanations. Perhaps she had already risen from the dead. She may have been biding her time in the tomb, waiting for the Last Judgment. Or more realistically, she was trapped at the bottom of the well, with all the mothers.

Dad withdrew for the rest of the day then flew to Scotland for the funeral, traveling more than nine thousand miles to see his mother in an open casket, to get a glimpse of the corpse that he had crawled out.

When he came back, he told me *the funeral was very nice.* Gran was buried in a new dress she had bought especially for the occasion; *it was very expensive.* I asked him if it was dark blue like all the others and he said no. *It was white, with bright-red roses.*

"Your gran wanted something bright, which she could see in the darkness of her coffin," he said, opening up a suitcase. "When you're buried," he said, "you wear very smart clothes, because when you die every day is so special."

My gran's airmail letters stopped arriving.

Dad put her old letters in his drawer in the bedroom dresser, where he kept his pipe and tobacco. He slipped in that photo of me and Gran, inside a prayer missal.

Sometimes I would steal into the bedroom and open the drawer and look at the photo. Those two foreigners. I would start to read the letters, but faced with the difficulty of her handwriting, I would soon give up.

The dead can't write, or there is no return address. But they can reach you in your dreams.

Not long after her death, I dreamed I was sitting on my grandma's lap. She was wearing the dress with the roses, kissing me on the cheek. Corpses are cold, this is true, but Gran was more demonstrative now that she was dead. I was less scared of her. Death seemed to be her . . . natural state.

Life is just a process of disintegration, she whispered sweetly in my ear.

Gran was the first person I ever knew who died. I still don't know much about her. Now and then Mom would bring Gran up; she spoke of her kindness, giving me another picture of this reserved woman. She told me about Gran's yearly trips to Lourdes; later in her life she went there twice a year. I never found out the exact hour of her death.

Every two years, my father goes to Scotland and visits his mother, but he has never mentioned her again.

If he's not careful, he'll take all his real feelings with him to the grave.

If I'm not careful, I will too.

Time dissolves everything: grandmothers, memories, feelings.

For most of my life, Margaret McCartney has been buried in consecrated ground, in the cemetery adjacent to the Cathedral of our Lady, gently disintegrating.

Even now, as I sit here with you, she's crumbling.

My grandma did not return from the dead. Her resurrection . . . did not happen.

Though it may happen yet.

I'm holding out for the occasion. But could you keep that to yourself?

It appears I didn't get through this quickly enough. The more you describe the dead, the faster they disintegrate. But time is so weird; it's like I just heard of Gran's death a minute ago and she just began decaying and I'm sitting at that kitchen table, starting to take it all in, sort it all out.

Holy Cross Cemetery, Part Two

Human, corpse, skeleton, dust: I think that's how it goes.

Work keeps me busy; I usually take lunch at my desk or between classes, but occasionally I treat myself and eat lunch at the cemetery. I like to sit on this bench in the shade of a scraggly palm tree, by the grave of Jack Haley, the guy who played the Tin Man in *The Wizard of Oz*, or was he the Scarecrow? He's just one of many actors buried at Holy Cross, names you would recognize and others who might have been well known in their day, like Sarah Allgood or Mona Darkfeather, but have since been forgotten.

I like to sit here—I mean there—and think about all sorts of things and well, one thing in particular.

That subject whose contemplation separates us from all the other clawed and declawed animals. A subject that eludes us: if you're not careful you could spend your entire life trying to catch the drift of death, scratching your head, until your scalp's all bloody. Until the day comes when your breathing stops and green fluids start to trickle out of your mouth and nostrils via the lungs.

But that's okay with me. You see, my mind has this nasty little habit of wandering, flying out of my body like a witch on a broomstick, clutching the handle with her thighs for dear life, but death gives me a purpose, a sense of direction. Death keeps me focused.

13

The Cycle of Experience

D___h, that word of Germanic origin, which is simultane-
ously a fact, an instance, a state, an action.

I'm not a very technical person. My understanding of the . . . physical
aspect of death is a little fuzzy and is in many ways limited to what I
knew as a child. I wrote a book report on the subject, copied straight
from the entry on "Death" in the encyclopedia. I can recall key aspects
of that report.

Death means the end of life. The heart stops beating and after that,
the brain is the first organ to go, something to do with the cells of the
cortex being susceptible to the end of the flow of blood and oxygen.
When we die, all our memories gurgle out of us; all our thoughts die
with us. It's as if the brain is relieved; that coordinating center of soft
nervous tissue that is said to have the consistency of hamburger meat can
finally stop wondering about death, speculating, fretting—the irresistible,
poetic practice of *thanatopsis*—and just . . . get on with it. The other
organs follow suit, bit by bit, cautiously, systematically.

The hair may continue to grow for several hours after death. Then it
stops, though I'm attached to my childish belief that the hair keeps
growing, not just for a few hours but for eternity: everyone in the afterlife
has long hair; the dead are no better than hippies, Death Metal heads,
Romantic composers. In some extreme cases, a skeleton's hair gets so
long it has been known to creep in the crack between the coffin lid and
the coffin and curl around the coffin's handles.

*Certain structures in the body are constantly decaying, dying, and being
replaced by new structures.* This is all part of something supposedly natural

14

called *the cycle of experience*. *Certain structures inside us die* while we're still trapped in the relative comfort of the womb. *Death completes the cycle.* I never figured out what these structures are exactly, but the implications of what I read and regurgitated onto paper stayed with me.

Robert

*In some cultures, alluding to the dead is considered taboo.
Even remembering them is forbidden. Above all, one must
never utter the deceased individual's name.*

Now that I think of it, I have known a couple more people who've died. First there was Robert. It's not like I knew him well or anything, but I did know him.

I used to work at this café in Santa Monica, Limbo, on Colorado and Thirteenth. This was the mid-1990s. I had moved to LA to be with this guy, Tim. The café doesn't exist anymore, but it had burnt-orange walls and dark wood tables with green lamps and battered velvet chairs and sofas. There was a lounge upstairs, where bands played. None of them were very good.

This woman Katarina ran the place. She had white-blonde hair and claimed she was descended from the missing daughter of the last Russian tsar, the one people thought had escaped execution. There were all those impostors; I hear they found the tsarevna's remains a couple of years ago. It was a good mystery while it lasted.

Katarina mainly hired foreigners—Russians and Israelis and South Africans and Poles; the accents were good for business. A few Americans worked there; Robert was one of them.

He wasn't much older than me, three, maybe four years? Tall and sturdy, he had long, dirty-blond hair and pale-blue eyes and big features. When I describe people, I feel awkward, like I'm giving a missing persons report, which I suppose in this case is exactly what I'm doing.

16

Robert was handsome; girls were always hitting on him at the café, coming up to the counter and saying, *Has anyone told you that you look like Brendan Fraser?* It's a dumb thing people do, using actors as a reference point, but all those girls were right; Robert bore a close resemblance to this actor. So close, that for a while he worked as a body double or stand-in.

I believe the difference between the two occupations is that a body double appears on camera, although his face is never shown, while a stand-in fills in for boring tasks that the actor doesn't want to do and that will never be seen, like lighting setup. Robert was even a stunt double once or twice—I think he got knifed. Eventually they replaced Robert because they found someone who looked even more like Brendan Fraser, whose movies are all pretty forgettable.

So I worked at Limbo four or five nights a week, 8:00 p.m. to 3:00 a.m. I could never do that now. These days I go to bed early.

Robert and I did the Friday night shift. When I got there, he would be sitting at the counter, counting in the drawer. We would say hi, and not much else. He wasn't much of a talker, and back then neither was I. I'm still pretty reserved. I don't know what got me talking to you.

Unlike you, Robert made me nervous. He often had this sort of amused expression on his face, or bemused—I reckon those two states are connected. It was like he was keeping a lot in.

Apart from the acting, the only real thing I knew about Robert was that he used heroin but was trying to stay clean. That's an important piece of information. Perhaps it's the only thing you need to know. Like I said, Robert was quiet, so someone else at work must have told me.

We would close at three, and then there was all the cleaning to do: fiddling with the fixtures on the espresso machine and scrubbing the grill, bleaching the sinks, sweeping and mopping, and counting out the drawer. Robert did the money and left me to do the bulk of the work. It was a question of seniority. He would slip twenty bucks or so from the

till. I'm not trying to soil his name. Just about everyone who worked
there took money. It was the only way the job made sense.

By the time we got out, it was usually around four. Robert drove
home. Or his girlfriend picked him up. She was Nordic; at first I thought
she was his sister. He would give her a big piece of chocolate cake. Neither
of them ever offered me a ride and I didn't have a car so I had to walk
down to Colorado and Third to catch the bus to the studio I was renting,
in the basement of this old building on Ashland. I worked out a deal
with a cab driver who was lonely and gave me free rides, but that came
later.

Not too long after I started working at Limbo, that boy from UCLA
disappeared. His picture was stapled to telephone poles all along Colorado. I took one of the missing posters down one night. The staples cut
my finger.

I've forgotten his name but I remember his face. He was a good-
looking kid, beautiful actually, short black hair, dark eyes, pale skin; he
was dressed formally in the photo, in a black suit with a white shirt and
black tie, the kind of suit you would wear to a prom or a funeral. He
had a pure smile. His picture was on my pinup board, but at some point
I filed it away.

I suppose I should have been slightly anxious, walking around by
myself late at night in a foreign city, near a neighborhood where a boy
had recently vanished, but for some reason it didn't overly concern me.

Robert got the bus with me, once or twice. He must have had car
trouble. He sat in front of me, listening to music on headphones. I wish
I could remember if we talked about anything on the way to the bus
stop. It was ten blocks, so we must have talked about something. Who
knows; maybe we didn't say a word to one another. We didn't want to
intrude on the quiet.

I mean, have you ever walked around Santa Monica at 4:00 a.m.?
It's so empty. Like being in outer space, if outer space had gas stations
and 7-Elevens and homeless people curled up in doorways. There was

one guy who lived a few doors down from the café. He didn't have legs, well, not complete ones. His legs ended at the knee. He had these cheap-looking silver prosthetics, but I never saw him wear them. He kept his silver legs neatly beside him. Everyone else was sleeping, but he was always awake.

That was my routine, or I should say our routine, for a few years. Then one Friday, I came into work and Robert wasn't there. The Hungarian girl, Reka, was counting in the drawer. Katarina was dropping off some supplies. I think I commented on the fact that Robert wasn't working and Katarina gave me a strange look.

"So you didn't hear?"

"Hear what?"

"Robert died."

That's about as much of the actual conversation I recall. Katarina filled me in on the details. Robert's girlfriend had gone out for the night, to stay with her parents, and Robert stayed in. When she came home the next day, she found Robert lying on the living room floor. He had OD'd. It seems he wanted to shoot up one last time, before he kicked dope for good. Just like all the others who want one more taste. His death was a question of either quantity or quality. He had shot up too much, or the stuff he bought must have been too strong, too pure.

I sort of understood why Robert . . . risked his life to have that experience. I tried dope when I was a teenager, just a couple of times—I tend to get hooked on things that have no substance, but I could see the appeal. The hype was fairly accurate; the effect was like bliss incarnate—once the puking was over. Like floating in the warmest, darkest sea imaginable, down in Hades or wherever. The nearest you could get to Death's rapturous oblivion, without the drawback of being stuck there. Coming down from the rush and that all-consuming sensation of . . . serenity—or do I mean stupefaction?—was like dying and being reincarnated, albeit into the same old worn-out self.

Still, I didn't believe it. How could Robert . . . stop, vanish, just like that? This was the emotion that overwhelmed all the others: disbelief. Is that even an emotion? Sometimes I get mixed up, trying to distinguish between my thoughts and my feelings. After Katarina told me, I started my shift. Everybody talked about it for the rest of the night. *Did you hear, did you hear?*

Katarina had a memorial for Robert at the café the week after he died. There was a good crowd, mostly staff and regulars. Robert's mom and girlfriend came; they sat together on one of the couches. I considered going up to them to convey my condolences. They were both very . . . subdued.

Memorials are odd occasions: people talking solemnly, laughing warily. At least at a funeral there is something to see, a corpse, or its reduction, even a casket; something material.

There was sadness floating around the room, but there was also an undertow of . . . excitement, the thrill, the flutter that accompanies the self-destruction of a fucked-up young man.

A few people spoke, but the only one I remember is Robert's aunt.

"Don't check out," she said. She was standing behind the counter, near the cake display case. We should assume she was wearing black. "Robert checked out, and all I can tell everyone here," she said, looking around, "especially those of you who are young and struggling with life, is don't do what Robert did. Don't check out."

This would have been 1998, August or September. Somehow, as I listened, I felt like Robert's death was an essential part of a decade that was nearly over, a late-century thread of young icons annihilating themselves—River Phoenix collapsing outside the Viper Room, Kurt Cobain blowing his brains out in Seattle, Richey Edwards *probably* jumping off the Severn Bridge in Wales, Jeff Buckley *accidentally* drowning in Wolf River, repeating the fate of his father, Tim Buckley, who was around the same age when he OD'd in the 1970s—so I guess every decade is a perfect time for the young to self-destruct.

Even though Robert wasn't an idol or a public figure, the aunt's words made quite an impression on me. Some words can do that. I've checked out frequently in my life, more than I care to remember, in more ways than I want to go into right now, but not permanently.

That afternoon I felt like I was part of something. I never feel that. Most of the time, it's like I'm a body double for myself, or a stand-in, and the real me is off . . . somewhere else. I'm experiencing this sensation right now with you. But at Robert's memorial, I felt like I was there.

A couple of days after the memorial, I had a little dream of Robert. Dreams are a chance for the dead to say hey, to let you know how they are. I had come to work, and Robert was counting in the drawer. The espresso machine was acting up; dark, wet espresso grounds were leaking everywhere.

"I thought you were dead," I said to Robert.

He looked up from his counting and began to explain that he hadn't died; his girlfriend had. There had been a mistake.

I was about to say that was it, that's all I have to tell you about Robert (it's not much, barely worth the telling), but I should mention something that happened a few months before Robert died. I wasn't going to, but I feel like I can tell you almost anything.

I ran into him by accident; actually, I found myself at his apartment. I . . . well, basically, I hooked up with this guy. I haven't done that in a long time, but I was restless when I was younger. I suspect I still have this restlessness inside me.

The guy lived in West LA, just off Venice Boulevard, in this pastel apartment complex. He was small and pale with black hair; he looked like the kid from UCLA, though not exactly, more like his brother, but there was something unusual about him, something . . . illegible in his dark-brown eyes.

Toward the end of our encounter, he looked up at me. "Want me to finish you off?"

I wasn't going to say no, but as he asked, I heard those words that had on every previous occasion been magic to my ears and for the first time ever I took them literally. When the guy swallowed me, he made a strange noise, guttural.

And it occurs to me now that when we die, when the world . . . swallows us, it's possible we'll feel intense pleasure, and, by extension, the world will also find the event of our death pleasurable. The world's pleasure might be even greater.

Afterward, the guy wouldn't let go. I had to practically . . . detach myself from him.

I left in a hurry and was feeling a bit jumpy, when whom should I run into, right outside the door, but Robert.

"Alistair?"

He looked confused. I must have looked confused too, though I couldn't see my own face. He was holding a dustpan and broom, like he had been doing some cleaning.

"What are you doing here?" he asked.

I said I was visiting a friend. But you know how in hookups you don't use real names? I gave him the name the guy had used, and Robert appeared to be even more mixed up. Then slowly, he got it.

"Oh, you mean Piotr?" There was that smile of his again.

"Oh yeah," I said, trying to wrangle my way out of it. I was startled. All my life I've felt I have to keep things hidden from everyone. As though I have these secrets that can't be revealed to anyone. Not that I know what my secrets are; most of them are concealed from me. Nevertheless, I sense this confidential material has changed over time and today is of a different nature.

But Robert was cool. "Hey, I'll walk out with you."

He went inside his apartment for a moment; he didn't invite me in. The door was ajar and I could see the place was very neat. A crème lounge. A glass coffee table. A glass dining table, some Impressiony prints, though I could be making that one up. Then he came out with a garbage bag and walked me down.

I've thought about that encounter a lot. In all the hundreds of thousands, possibly millions, of pastel condos in LA, I end up in the apartment next door to Robert. What are the odds?

I'm probably reading too much into it—I do that sometimes, see magical connections, find significance where there is none—but it reminds me of that Poe story "The Masque of the Red Death," one of my favorite stories as a kid. I haven't read it in years, but I seem to recall a prince holding a masked ball in his castle. There's a plague going on, so he has this party to take everyone's minds off death. His guests arrive and his servants bolt the doors, but Death finds his way in. Death comes disguised as himself. Everyone thinks it's a terrific and gruesomely realistic costume, but when the prince tries to rip the intruder's costume off, there's nothing beneath it, pure formlessness. The prince drops dead, along with all his friends.

It's like Robert was holed up in his condo, hiding out, then Death turned up and his own death began. But wait, that would mean I'm Death, so ignore what I said. Our encounter means nothing; there's nothing beneath it, raw chance, pure formlessness.

While Robert was alive, I worried that he might talk about me at work. But then Robert died. I think I felt a shred of relief that he took my secret with him.

Maybe that's why we bury people deep in the ground, to keep the things they know about us locked away. Or better yet, we cremate them, and at the same time burn this information.

Perhaps we should still be worried about the dead, the dirt they have on us. Perhaps we should be even more concerned about the dead than the living, what they know, the intimacies they could use against us.

Robert's been dead for almost thirteen years. The café's been closed almost as long. I hadn't thought about it in ages, but then I saw Katarina on the street the other day. She had the same white-blonde hair. I pretended not to see her and I don't think she saw me, unless she was also pretending.

Anyway, seeing her reminded me of Robert. His funeral was on a boat. I had a prior engagement, but I remember Katarina told me his girlfriend sang the Kaddish beautifully; she didn't know she had such a lovely voice. Robert was cremated and scattered at sea, in the Santa Monica Bay.

How long do you think it took for his ashes to disappear? They must have floated for a while, before the fish got to them, with their unblinking eyes, their mouths in a constant state of opening and closing. Robert's ashes must have drifted before they settled in the bellies of a thousand fish. Like Jonah in the whale, but dispersed and distributed among sea creatures of various shapes and sizes, all over the Pacific.

Thirteen years, that's a considerable length of time. I wonder how Robert feels about his scattered state? Most likely, he doesn't feel anything; there's no trace of Robert anymore, but bear with me. Does he miss the world and its requirements? Does he miss doing boring activities like cleaning? Did he acclimate to nothingness quickly, or did it take some adjusting? Was he at home immediately; was the void what he wanted all along? I mean, how long does it take to get used to being nothing?

The Dead Man's Things

Never borrow anything from the dead. Destroy their belongings,
or they'll come looking for those possessions eventually.

My memory is blurry to the point that you should not trust me, but I recall the first time I became . . . aware of death.

I was five, going on six. I was in the backyard, doing nothing, or nothing visible to the eye—basically wandering around and daydreaming—when my dad came home. He had been on a gardening job for some rich old lady. I saw that the car was full of boxes, and when he got out I asked what was in them.

He told me that the husband of his client had *passed away*—that phrase again, a sentence we say over and over—and she had given him her husband's clothes to donate to St. Vincent de Paul. Dad opened up the back of the car to grab his cooler and went inside, so I began to investigate.

The boxes contained the clothes of an old man, attire from another era: porkpie hats, black dress shoes, argyle socks, suspenders, ties with tiepins, starched shirts with the cuff links in the holes in the cuffs, and dark suits with pinstripes fine as the strings that manipulate the limbs of puppets. The clothes were pristine, though a few of the white shirts had faint brown stains in the underarms.

I doubt if I fully comprehended what I was touching, but the clothes drew me in. There was something magical about these garments. It was as if our off-white station wagon had been transformed into a pale hearse. I sensed the man had gone somewhere where he didn't need all his things, so he left them behind, like a snake sheds its skin.

25

There was one small box, black with a company's name in gold lettering. I opened it up. In the box were five pairs of glasses. I picked up a pair of black horn-rims and put them on as my mom came up behind me.

"Don't wear those," she said, snatching the glasses away. "You might catch something."

I don't know what she thought I would catch. Some eye disease, I suppose. The more I think about it—and I think of those dead guy's clothes at least once a week—my mother wasn't concerned with contagion or infection. I suspect it was a more general superstition she had in mind, that it's bad luck to wear the glasses of the dead, that if you put their glasses on it will wreak havoc with your vision: you might see something only the dead should see.

Orientation

Whom were you waiting for at the cemetery gates? It's almost like you were waiting for me.

It's so easy to get lost at Holy Cross. The first time I took a look around, after my lunch, it was one of those June Gloom days. Many of the headstones are made from pale-yellow stone, and I felt like I was walking through a giant filing cabinet crammed with manila folders. The graves all looked the same, just names and dates and slender epitaphs as far as my eye could see. The clipped lawns and the rows and rows of identical gravestones with former humans tucked away behind them began to give me a whirling sensation that is commonly known as vertigo and usually the result of looking down from a great height, so I left.

I had learned my lesson, so the next time I got a map from a lady at the information booth near the entrance. The map had an alphabetical key indicating the burial sections' names: *A, Immaculate Conception*; *C, Precious Blood*; *T, The Assumption*; which is not far from *V, Visitation*. Next to the key were two blank grids, with numbers and letters running down the sides, which, I gathered, were meant to help you locate specific individuals. They reminded me of cryptic crossword puzzles waiting to be filled in, puzzles that come without clues or instructions.

The lady at the information booth seemed distracted when I went back to ask her some questions about the layout—perhaps she was pondering the certain prospect of being subtracted from the world and becoming an abstraction, until we exist in the heads of our loved ones only as vague . . . ideas, though who knows: sometimes I think you would have better luck reading the mind of a corpse than another living human being—and the maintenance men in their tight blue uniforms were just as unhelpful.

Undeterred, I walked around, and found myself in a section where the headstones were matte black and speckled, resembling well-used leather wallets holding miscellaneous forms of currency. I noticed some graves had the date of death in the upper right corner, right where you place the date in a letter. Others didn't bother with the birth date, as if being born didn't matter. I had that warm feeling you get on your skin when you're out strolling in the open air, calm and rosy as an apple, but the day was muggy, and the dates of strangers' deaths accumulated and I walked until my legs were achy and my head felt glazed and hollow.

Since then, I've tried to pace myself. I still have the map; see, it's creased yet has been of no use. Even if you can read it, the tin markers sticking out of the grass, indicating the numbers of rows and graves, are so small and faded, and often they're not even there. It's as though the cemetery is determined to give visitors as little information as possible, to keep us from finding anyone or anything.

Mike Hazelwood
and the Floor of the Dead

A death has occurred or is near:

Then there was Mike. I made Mike's acquaintance in October 1995, the week I arrived in LA. I had only been here a couple of days. I'm pretty certain he was the first person I got to know, the first friend I made. Though I use that term lightly. I'm not what you would call a great friend. I still spell the word incorrectly, putting the *e* before the *i*.

So we met at Highways, this theater in an old warehouse in an industrial part of Santa Monica, just off Olympic.

I was taking a workshop of Tim's, a movement workshop. I wouldn't be caught dead doing that now, but dance or something approximating dance was a practice I dabbled in back then.

When Tim and I got to the theater, it would have been around five. Mike was sitting on a sofa in the lobby, reading a paper. I don't think Tim knew him either, and we all chatted a little. I don't recall too much about that first meeting. Although it was fall, I had managed to get sunburnt. I felt self-conscious, about the sunburn, about everything. Tim told Mike I had just come to LA from London, which is where I had been living for a year or two.

"Ah, welcome, welcome," Mike said.

He must have been around fifty, but he was like a gawky, gray-haired teenager, tall and rangy with a nervous laugh. He had a weird mangled accent, similar to how mine sounds now. Mike told us he was from England but had been living in the States for many years, and had spent good chunks of time in Australia. He felt very . . . familiar. Kind of like you. You remind me of someone, whose name is, as the saying goes, on the tip of my tongue.

I was closely observing myself but I do remember being struck by Mike's last name. *Hazelwood*, like a forest of hazelnut trees. One of those old English names that is derived from the locale, the place of birth. Way back in Mike's genealogy, the first Hazelwood must have lived near a forest. Even though he had died and the family had moved away, the name remained the same. Centuries had passed and here was Mike Hazelwood living far from England, far from that forest, in California, by the sea.

That fall I saw Mike every week.

He always came to the workshops early, and I would come down to say hi. I was staying at Highways, temporarily, in this attic that was Tim's office. I wasn't meant to be there so I had to keep a low profile and avoid the landlord, a pale woman with red hair, but I could see who was in the lobby through a hole in the wall.

"Hey man," Mike would say, "how's it going?" On cooler days he wore this big black coat. I would sit down next to him on that shabby sofa and we'd talk, but apart from his greeting, I couldn't tell you the content of our conversations. I've never been a good listener; I'm too wrapped up in the conversation in my own head, which is far more compelling.

Yet I can still hear, faintly, his way of talking, slowly and hesitantly, as if he didn't trust the words that were forming in his mouth, as if he was apprehensive of everything he was saying.

You got this sense from Mike that he was extremely uncomfortable, not just speaking, but in his own body. He shared with me once that he was taking the workshop to overcome this discomfort.

It was quite painful to watch him participate in the movement exercises. Mike's lumbering gestures were reminiscent of Lurch, the manservant from *The Addams Family*, though Mike was not quite so graceful. As Mike shifted his limbs, his skeleton and skin appeared to be at odds with one another. Still wearing his black coat, his jerky motions and grim expression of concentration made him look like a man dancing at his own funeral.

I'm not one to talk; when one of my workshop partners would try to manipulate my body, I would tense up, like a corpse attempting to resist the advances of a mortician. But Mike took each step so seriously, as if eventually this would pay off and from within his clumsy pirouetting his spirit or soul would show through.

He was goofy too, with the spacey, scattered air of someone who took far too much acid in the '60s, crucial brain cells dissolved from one hit too many; every now and then, as he moved, he would break into laughter.

I lived at Highways for about six or eight months, rent-free. That period of life is indistinct to me now, but then I'm not sure what period of life isn't.

I was dazed, still wondering how I had ended up in LA, which had never been on my radar and struck me as an endless, bleached-out sequence of condos and spindly palm trees.

I would hang out by myself in the attic, which was cozy in a musty sort of way. There was a fridge and a futon and a big old desk. There wasn't a microwave but there was a kettle, so I could make cups of soup. Tim bought me these purple curtains with a moon pattern and a string of lights in the shape of little chilies to brighten up the place.

Things between Tim and I were . . . volatile. Our passion would send us into a kind of . . . hole. There were intervals when he needed time out.

When I got antsy I would go wandering. The neighborhood was deserted, just factories and warehouses with an odd house here and there. There was a park a couple of blocks away, frequented by hookers and dealers. I would sit in the kids' spaceship in the park and watch the deals, the exchanges. I felt . . . invincible, like you do when you're twenty-three.

Once in a while, as I walked back to the theater, cars would slow down and I would receive invitations from strangers.

What I recall most of that time is a feeling of being unsure of myself and somewhat . . . uncontrollable. This feeling never left me. In that attic and on those vacant streets, I discovered a number of things about who I was, they were incredibly profound, but unfortunately I've forgotten what those attributes were.

If I wasn't in the mood to talk to Mike before the workshop, I would stay upstairs. Sometimes I would watch him through that hole in the office wall, reading his paper or checking out an exhibition in the gallery. But he was more drawn to the gallery's concrete floor.

The floor was covered with an art project, outlines of bodies drawn in permanent marker, like the outlines they draw on the pavement when someone jumps from a skyscraper. These outlines were filled in with names, thousands of names, of people who had died of AIDS. Most patrons ignored the names, but Mike would get down on his hands and knees and inspect the names, really read them.

I would watch him until I got bored.

As soon as Tim turned up, I'd head down to the workshop. To start things off, we would all form a circle, which I believe is meant to serve a protective, magical function.

I was the only person living in the theater, which in a previous life had been a munitions factory and after that a factory where they manufactured spoons—not regular spoons but the musical kind. This guy Lawrence Welk owned the plant; he had this corny variety TV show, where his band played and guests yodeled and tap danced, but I hear the spoons are how he made his fortune.

During the day it was fine, but at night, it got to me, especially if I came back late from work or wandering, or woke up and had to go take a leak. The bathroom was at the other end of the space. To get to it, I had to walk through the gallery and bring a flashlight to guide me.

I felt superstitious about treading on the names, so I would try and tiptoe around them, like avoiding cracks in the sidewalk, but it was impossible. There were so many names, inside the bodies, spilling over their outlines. Whenever I stepped on someone's name I would say *sorry, sorry*. I would start to imagine all those names were whispering to me, repeating their own name over and over, above the low whir of assembly lines run by the ghosts of munitions workers and the feeble clacking of musical spoons.

By the time I got to the auditorium, lit only by a ghost light, the exposed light in a small wire cage that is kept on when a theater is empty, the light whose purpose is both practical and supernatural, I had pretty much psyched myself out.

One night, I accepted an invitation from one of those strangers in their cars. He was curious about the place, and I grabbed my flashlight and showed him around. He had spiky blond hair with dark roots showing. He was wearing black jeans, a studded belt, that Dalí skull T-shirt, the one where the skull is a bunch of naked women in careful formation. I shone my light on the gallery floor.

"Spooky," he said.

He took off his shirt, and in the weak glow of my torch I admired the tattoo of Santa Muerte on his chest, the tip of her scythe grazing his left nipple. As we stood on those names, we kissed. Overcoming my superstitions, I pushed him facedown onto the concrete floor.

The next day I apologized to the names and my knees were bruised.

Look, I know I keep returning to myself and avoiding my subject, which is meant to be Mike, because I didn't make the effort to get to know him. He wasn't fascinating or beautiful enough to hold my attention.

I'm sure I'll have to pay for this down the line. Isn't there a circle in *The Inferno* where the superficial ones go?

After the workshop ended, we saw Mike from time to time.

Tim and I even went over to Mike's once, a fancy ocean front apartment in Malibu. It took us ages to find parking.

Mike made us dinner and played us some songs on the piano. I had learned he was a songwriter; Tim probably told me. Mike had penned a couple of famous tunes, including the song "It Never Rains in Southern California." That's how he made his fortune, music royalties.

I spent my childhood glued to the radio; in our house the easy listening station was always on, but I didn't know that song. The title, yes, but not the words or the melody. I don't remember those tunes Mike played for us either; my mind was . . . elsewhere, though I do recollect his voice was flat.

Afterward, he walked us to our car. I think we all commented on the sea air. Mike was so tall he had to stoop over to give me a hug. Like all his other gestures, his embrace was ungainly. Yet full of so much feeling, as if you might be crushed by a combination of his physical strength and his . . . emotions, which were threatening to overflow, and there was that nervous laugh again, like he was flustered by his own intensity.

Mike died of a heart attack, on the sixth of May 2001. At the time of his death he wasn't in LA; he was in Italy, Florence. I heard from a mutual friend that Mike died in a hotel bed in the middle of the night.

What an odd way to die—not the heart attack, not the bed or the night, but while you're on vacation. As if Mike went to Florence specifically for that purpose, traveled thousands of miles to meet his death, which required a beautiful location.

But when he woke up with a start and . . . realized what was going on, he must have felt scared to be dying so far from home, in a foreign land. Dying is already like going to a foreign land, the most foreign of lands, where you know no one, even though everyone is there.

A month or so after Mike's death, a postcard came in the mail. Post-marked Florence, April 29. The picture was a painting by Caravaggio, one of his voluptuous street urchins transformed through art into something holy: a pale young man with black curly hair, his curls entangling with the dark background, his face shining out of the darkness.

Mike had written on the back about having seen this painting, how magnificent it was. I couldn't read the rest of his scrawl, though there was an *x* and an *o* at the end. And a *wish you were here.*

For a while Tim and I entertained the idea of how weird this was, like the postcard had been sent from the afterlife. But we knew it had just gotten lost; Italy's mail service is notoriously slow.

I discovered a couple of things about Mike, *after the fact.* I just wasn't interested while he was alive. People get my attention far more easily when they're gone.

So I looked him up online, one night when I wasn't sure what to do with myself. Most humans use the Internet to interact with the living, but I prefer to use it to connect with the dead. I don't mean like in a séance. I just read up on them, though if there were a space you could make contact with the dead, the Internet, ethereal and nowheresy as it is, like a high-tech Ouija board, might be a good place to start.

The *Wikipedia* entry on Mike had a fairly extensive biography, information about his music and composing, and a list of the songs he's written. Most of the titles were unfamiliar to me, except for "The Air That I Breathe," which I vaguely know. At the bottom of the page, after the references, Mike's name was listed under these *related categories*: *20th century English songwriters, 1941 births, 2001 deaths, and deaths from myocardial infarction*, which I guess is the technical term for heart attack.

Apart from that, there wasn't much about him. A German music blog had a retrospective article on Mike's career. I didn't bother to translate it. The site seemed rather obscure, but I suppose we don't get to be picky about where we're memorialized. If we're documented by even one amateur, archived in a little nook or dusty corner of cyberspace, we're insanely lucky.

On Google Images there were a few scattered photos, mainly from the 1960s, when Mike was young and in this garage band the Breathers. In one shot, the band members were wearing ruffled paisley shirts, running through a field of flowers. It was all very *groovy*, a term Mike used, I'm sure of it, during our lost conversations.

In another, Mike was dressed like a Quaker, black suit and black broad-brimmed hat, white shirt with a pointy collar, looking as sharp as Death himself, wearing mirrored shades, so I couldn't see his blue eyes: I didn't mention that Mike often seemed to be squinting, like he could only take a small portion of the world in at any given time.

I listened to one of the band's songs, "When Tomorrow Comes Tomorrow." It was upbeat, the lyrics naïvely hopeful, but the sound of this utopian anthem was muffled and distorted, like it had been recorded in the bowels of the Underworld.

That was the extent of my discoveries.

I'm not definite on where Mike's body ended up. Was he buried in Florence? Was his corpse flown back in cargo to California? Or was he shipped to his place of birth, so he could be buried beneath those hazelnut trees, which hopefully had not been cut down?

I think what I've been telling you is a kind of eulogy, though one that fails: it sheds no light on the man it's dedicated to, it eclipses or negates him.

This could be a eulogy for anyone, for no one.

I don't think much about Mike, except in passing. Occasionally, a memory returns to me: one afternoon, not long before the landlord with the red hair found my stuff and kicked me out, I observed Mike through the hole in the wall as he was inspecting the floor of the dead. With the swiftness of a magician, he pulled out a magic marker from a pocket of his black coat and, hunched over, began freshening up some of the names that were fading, tracing over each letter with real care.

Next to Mike's name on his *Wikipedia* page there's an [*edit*] icon. The word is italicized and placed in square brackets, like death italicizes and brackets us, like death edits us, emends us, or is *edit* just a nicer way of saying *delete*? I could go in and modify his page myself, though *every addition requires a verifiable citation* and none of my anecdotes can be substantiated. That popular reference site is stricter with this rule around living persons. It's easier to alter and rewrite articles about the dead, as is often the case.

Mike's . . . accessible as information, stored and transmitted in the form of electronic signals.

However, the things that genuinely interest me about him aren't available. They're in a . . . space where there are no categories, no signals, no data.

During my most recent search for Mike, I found myself looking up the afterlife instead and came to an empty *Wikipedia* page that said nothing but *"After death," "Life after death,"* and *"Hereafter" redirect here.*

When I die, when it's my turn to be categorized and filed away, perhaps the first person to greet me will be Mike. He'll be sitting on a thread-bare sofa in the afterlife's crummy lobby, and he'll receive me in his typically awkward manner. No, he'll have gained more confidence, feel more at home, more himself amid Death's dark psychedelia.

"Hey man, you finally made it!" he'll say, patting the couch. "Come sit next to me."

I'll sit down and apologize for not listening to Mike sing those songs of his that night in Malibu, and he'll go, "Look man, no worries. I can play them for you later." He'll tell me about the band he has formed, Mike Hazelwood and the Floor of the Dead. They only play one song, he'll explain, the one about breathing air, which sounds unbelievably groovy in a realm where you can't breathe. He won't have lost his sense of humor or his sweet quality, despite Death's bleakness.

I'll apologize a second time for not really getting to know him when he was alive or dead, and he'll say, "That's okay. We've got plenty of time now. More time than we'll know what to do with. Let me show you around."

He'll pull out a flashlight, necessary to illuminate Death's darkness. He'll suddenly look more somber. Mike will take me by the hand and whatever Death actually *is* will get underway.

The California Section

I don't want to disturb the dead. I don't want the dead to hear me; they'll hold every word against me. Is that why I'm talking this quietly?

I was planning on reading the newspaper, but let me put it away.

The *Los Angeles Times* is not an especially good paper, but I like the California section. It amounts to six pages, folds up nicely in my back pocket, yet it's very informative. It's where they have the stories of local interest, which are for the most part violent little stories of the intentional or accidental ways people died. You only have to read the titles to get the gist of them: *Train Kills Woman in Tunnel*; *Boy Mauled to Death by Dogs*; *Man Swept out to Sea*. Or if you're like me, you can read further.

You can learn about the guy who went hunting in Riverside County on New Year's Day. He caught some geese, but one fell into a frigid pond. The man dove in to retrieve his goose. His body was found at the bottom of the pond, weighed down by too many rounds of ammunition, but his red hunting cap was floating on the surface.

Then there was the homeless man who was sitting at the corner of Third and Berendo in the Mid-Wilshire District, in front of one of that neighborhood's prestigious art deco apartment buildings, when a stranger came up to him, poured gasoline on his head, and set him alight, the motivation appearing to be *personal dislike of the homeless*. The gasoline can was red, just like the hunter's cap. The victim was rushed to the hospital, where he was listed as *death-imminent*.

And take the boy arrested by the Lost Hills Police Department. His story came in installments. Released from the station at midnight, *wearing only a thin T-shirt and a pair of cotton shorts*, he wandered off into the dark; disoriented, he fell down a ravine. Investigators didn't locate his remains, a skull and a ribcage, until a year later. It took more time to unearth the rest of his skeleton, which had been scattered over an area of five miles in seemingly random patterns by the bush's disparate collection of wild animals.

You can keep on reading and marvel at all the ways people can die. The poor guy who was trying to climb into the grounds of the Playboy Mansion and fell from a tree —or did the branch break from his weight?— managed to enter the grounds but was *pronounced dead at the scene*. The grandma in Echo Park who stopped to talk to a neighbor on a Sunday morning—she was asking if she could borrow some sugar— and was *promptly crushed to death by the crown of a rotten palm tree*; she became debris pressed beneath debris. The corpse that was minding its own business in the trunk of a taxi impounded for parking violations in a tow yard in downtown LA, until an employee *noticed something seeping from the trunk*. Bound with duct tape, the victim appeared to have suffocated. *The well-traveled professor* in Marina del Rey who had been sitting out on his balcony for five days, dead with a self-inflicted gunshot to his eye. Neighbors mistook him for a Halloween display, until *they heard popping noises* and some goo dripped onto the balcony below.

On the next page are the military deaths, young men with bright smiles and tight fades killed by fanatics bearing weaponry of idiosyncratic designs or blown to bits by improvised explosive devices that are either sophisticated or crude. After that come the obituaries, those brief reports on individuals who died *peacefully* or *unexpectedly* from old age or God's long list of diseases. The word *obituary* comes from the Latin *obitus*: departure, encounter, a going to meet. The word *Deaths* is at the top of the page, in a Gothic-style font, but the obituaries themselves are in plain script that's so tiny you have to squint.

As I read it strikes me that there are only so many ways to be born.

But when it comes to death, God is at his most imaginative; death is where he gets creative. Although dying has its methods and its categories that reoccur, the range of death on offer to us is plentiful: natural or unnatural, gentle or violent, at the hands of someone else or by your own hand. The options are as varied as the weather—local, national, global—that appears on the back of the California section. The options seem to be infinite.

Though of course death's not an option. It's a condition: *The individual hereby agrees that God or Death can come along any time he or it wants, in any guise, by any means of transportation, and, depending on their mood, destroy us swiftly or in a more leisurely fashion.* The inevitability of death, your death and mine, is laid out in a hidden clause in the contract of existence that is binding, a clause written in God's handwriting, which is even tinier than the obits, so everyone overlooks it.

Usually, by the time I'm through reading—the newspaper, I mean—I feel dizzy with possibility, and I've got black newsprint all over my fingers.

A Tour

The cemetery's blandness is periodically disrupted: Rita Hayworth's headstone is carved from a blue-black marble and gives off a deep shimmer. Lawrence Welk's bears an image of a man holding a baton, treble and bass clefs whirling across the stave behind him. Hayworth's grave is glamorous; Welk's is jazzy enough to be blasphemous, though he was said to be very devout.

Despite the cemetery's efforts to dissuade me, I have familiarized myself with the grounds.

If I were to take you by the hand and give you a tour of some of my favorite spots, I would start by showing you the Grotto; it's an artificial cave, made out of actual volcanic rock, a reconstruction of the grotto at Lourdes. Inside there's a statue of the Virgin Mary, and outside one of Saint Bernadette, hands clasped, gazing at the Virgin in awe, just like Bernadette must have gazed when she saw the actual Virgin at Lourdes, or thought she saw her, right before the Virgin told her to eat the dirt to find the holy water and gave her all those other unconventional instructions and everyone thought the poor girl was crazy. Unlike Bernadette's ecstatic expression, the statue of the Virgin looks sort of indifferent to the miracle of her own visitation.

I like it inside the cave; it's mossy and cool and you can barely hear the traffic. There's a table of novena candles people have lit for the souls of the dead. It's said that one candle takes a year off someone's stint in Purgatory. That's one of our years, which is the equivalent of one second down or over there. But you have to breathe lightly so as not to extinguish the flames, and after a while a cave tends to get damp and chilly, so we'd leave and head to the grave of Bela Lugosi, in the Grotto section, lot 120, plot #1, a brown headstone with a black border and a crucifix and rose etched into the left corner. *Beloved Father 1882–1956.*

I stumbled on his grave. Someone had left a bright-red rose for Lugosi, on the image of the rose, which you could still see behind the real flower, just as you can still see death peeping out from behind a corpse, which is real but a kind of representation. Lugosi was well aware of this: as a young soldier in the Hungarian army, he hid in a mass grave and played dead—he claimed this is how he learned to act. He's buried in the black silk cape he wore in his vampire movies, but everyone knows that; I wonder if it has shredded by now? I'm not so clear on the rate of silk's disintegration.

From there, we would go to the Resurrection area, and the grave of Darby Crash, tier 9, plot #115. It's nowhere near as prestigious a location. The grass is brown and dry, not lush and green like in some other sections. Crash's real name is etched into the dull-beige stone, *JAN PAUL BEAHM 1958–1980*, his stage name incised below in lowercase letters, surrounded by an engraving of brown rosary beads, an unwitting reference to the rosary of little red circles that looped around his neck and cascaded down his collarbone, the cigarette burns he stubbed out on his skin, or encouraged fans to do the same when he sang with the Germs, right up until the night he intentionally OD'd in the Spanish stucco house in Hollywood, allegedly scrawling *Here Lies Darby* on the bedroom wall in his own blood and laying down beneath the words, right where they found him, the phrase functioning as both an epitaph and a caption.

It would be time to get out of the sun, so we'd walk up to the Risen Christ Mausoleum and work up a sweat. Avoiding the chapel with its stained-glass monstrosities, we'd take a right to the main room, where they have the marble crypts and crematory niches, in vertical rows of six and twelve, respectively. It's not unlike being in a bank vault, with its walls of safe deposit boxes to secure items of extreme value, or just a regular post office, an airy room of PO boxes, containing packages people didn't want delivered to their home.

I would direct your attention to the crypt of Jimmy Durante, block #35, crypt F2. It's indistinguishable from the others, an inscription in plain gold lettering and a gold cross at the top, so small it seems like an afterthought, though the swirls and veins in the marble break up the monotony. Maybe I'd tell you the joke about his cremation. I forget how it goes exactly, but the punch line has to do with his conspicuous nose, how they couldn't burn it, no matter how many times they sent it back to the furnace. So they finally gave up and popped his schnoz in with the ash.

We would end the tour outside with Sharon Tate, who can be found in the Saint Anne's section, lot 152, plot #6, nestled behind a gray headstone that used to be black. In the center, Jesus holds his hands out in supplication, so you can see the holes where the nails went in. There's only the year of Tate's death inscribed, *1969*, not the month or the date, perhaps a deliberate omission, a way to erase the coordinates of Tate in space and time when the Manson Family dropped into her house on Cielo Drive and, per Charles's instructions, proceeded to *totally destroy everyone . . . as gruesome as you can.*

Tate's been down there for forty-two years, longer than I've been around up here, her little baby skeleton perched in her arms, the one that was inside her, the one Sadie Atkins couldn't bring herself to cut out. In her acid-inflected testimony, Sadie spoke of Tate's *rapidly changing facial expressions and her pretty paisley bikini and ropes and carving forks and peace to infinity and the thought of a living being in there blowing my mind.* We don't have Tate's account of that night—the dead have escaped language, discarded it—though in an interview shortly before she died, she said that she felt her *entire life had been governed by fate, fate blows my mind,* adopting the same rhetoric as her killer. Do you think everyone's hair turns gray in death, or is Tate a skeleton with long blonde hair curled around bones that are even blonder?

As a tour, mine wouldn't be all that different from the standard Hollywood tours of graves of the stars, though not as comprehensive. I'm just a guide with some grave locators who can share some morbid trivia.

You would probably get a better sense of my experience of Holy Cross by sitting beside me on the bench beneath the raggedy palm tree, as I touch the bench's wood to keep the Destroyer at bay and tell you a few of the ideas and stories that are swirling in my head.

The Birnies

I used to live near death. Well, not far from it.

If you wanted to drop in on the Birnies, all you had to do was head out the front door of our house in Willagee, take a right, walk down Wheyland Street, then, before you got to Leach Highway, take the short footpath that leads to Moorhouse Street. David and Catherine Birnie lived at the end of that footpath in a pale-blue asbestos house.

I must have walked down that path a thousand times when I was a kid. I would pass the blue house and walk a little further, to the park or the deli or the fish and chip shop or the cake shop for the brief time it was there. The shops were about a ten-minute walk. From our front door to the Birnies' front door couldn't have taken more than four minutes.

In 1986, in the months of October and November, Catherine and David Birnie abducted, raped, tortured, and murdered four young women.

I've retained the particulars, assembled facts and factoids from all manner of places, pieced together fragments from the reaches of my own memory.

But let's go back to the start, before we knew what was going on, or who was doing what, before the Birnies were caught.

That spring—remember, seasons are inverted in Australia—girls were disappearing in quick succession.

The names and dates: Mary Neilson vanished on October 6. Susannah Candy disappeared on October 20. Noelene Patterson vanished on the first of November. Denise Brown was last seen on November 6.

Every day it was in the papers: the dates, the names, out-of-focus photographs of the young women's faces. Details: Noelene's car was abandoned on Canning Highway; it appeared she had run out of petrol. Mary's library books from the university—psychology textbooks, including Freud's *Interpretation of Dreams*—were found scattered on the esplanade in Perth. Denise had been dancing all night at The Stoned Crow in North Fremantle; she came with friends but decided to make her own way home. Susannah sent letters to her parents, professing *she was okay* and *not to worry*, but her dad didn't believe them; there was something questionable about the slant of his daughter's handwriting.

People were fearful. The papers warned women *not to be out alone at night*. My sister Julianne was studying pharmacology, taking evening classes at the same university that Mary attended; Julianne waited at the same bus stop Mary was last seen at on Stirling Highway.

At first, my sister wore her white lab coat; she thought it made her look less appealing. But then she worried it attracted attention, the bright whiteness of the coat, so she took it off and stuffed it in her bag before she left the building.

Naturally, Julianne was distressed when it turned out that it wasn't just a man abducting the girls but a couple, and this couple lived nearby.

Imagine if they had offered her a ride: *Oh you live in Willagee too, Woodhams Street? We live right around the corner from you! Isn't that funny! What a coincidence! Why wait by yourself when you can drive with us? No, it's no trouble, no trouble at all.*

Unlike my sister, when I came home from school that day and heard it was our neighbors who had been killing the girls, I wasn't upset. The Birnies wouldn't have been interested in a boy like me.

I was about to use a term from adolescence and say that *I was so spun out*, but this would imply there was stress attached, and that's not true either.

I'm not sure what the right word is to convey how I felt knowing something like this was going on just around the corner, while I was doing my homework, watching TV, dreaming.

Like in every good crime story, we slept with the doors unlocked and the windows open.

So what ended the Birnies' spree, or *our dark adventure*, as David Birnie referred to it in the *West Australian*?

There was a fifth young woman, who got away. Colleen Sheir was abducted *at knifepoint* by the Birnies, Sunday night, November 9. The couple drove her *at knifepoint* to their home. The next morning, she escaped through a window. *That lucky girl*, as the paper referred to her, *saved by a knock on the door, ran naked through the park, the grass still wet with dew*, straight to the local fish and chip shop. The owner *was just getting the fryer going*. The girl snatched up some newspapers to cover herself, those papers filled with stories of all the disappearing girls, and began to tell him her story, in fits and starts. *She began to weep*, not about her predicament *but because of the thorns embedded in the soles of her feet*, from the park's harsh grass. The police were called and, in a dark-blue dressing-gown that was far too big for her, Colleen led them back to the pale-blue asbestos house.

In custody, when it became clear the game was over, both Catherine and David were surprisingly talkative.

Their technique was as follows: they would offer the woman a ride, or ask for directions. Catherine's presence made it easier to lure women near or into their car—a 1971 emerald-green Toyota.

Once the women were in the car—*make sure you put on your seatbelt; it's the law, you know*—the couple would pull their knives out of nowhere, like magicians.

In the bedroom their props included chains, sleeping pills, more knives, gags, nylon cords, cocaine. David Birnie injected his genitals with coke or anesthetic to keep *his member* numb, *so the act of rape could be repeated.* Catherine Birnie was always in the bed, a queen-size with an antique headboard, sometimes *participating*, sometimes *just observing.*

Ideally, the couple liked to keep the girls alive for several days, then, *when it was time, when they were done,* they would kill the girls with knives and hands and pills and nylon cords and bury them in the pine forests, not the one near Willagee (which, incidentally, means *place of pines*) but the more remote forests on the northern outskirts of Perth.

One stubborn girl they thought was dead kept sitting up in her grave. *Kind of like Rasputin*, David was quoted as saying, alluding to the mad Russian monk who, despite cyanide-laced wine and cakes, numerous shots to his body, and blunt force trauma to the head, refused to die.

Rasputin finally drowned, in a frozen river. David finished his victim off with an axe, or was it a shovel?

The police found pine needles in the car, all over the house, even in the couple's bedding. In the station's transcripts, Catherine talked at length about the pine needles, how annoying they were, how difficult they were to get rid of, *how they got in absolutely everything.*

Reporters had a field day, combing through the fine points, coming up with their theories, analyzing the colorful aspects of the case.

David Birnie worked in a wrecker's yard: *Was it just coincidence,* one article asked, *that this man who made his living not by fixing cars but by dismantling them, breaking automobiles down into their components, also liked to take apart young women?*

And what was the meaning of the torn-out picture of Rasputin taped to the refrigerator? Did Mr. Birnie fancy himself as some kind of depraved mystical healer?

Another article focused on Catherine: *How could a mother of seven from a previous marriage perpetrate such evil?* The writer played up her role in the murders, positioning her as the mastermind. After all, when police asked David why he had committed the crimes, he responded, *Because of this book Catherine showed me.*

A few years back, she had introduced him to the Marquis de Sade's *120 Days of Sodom*; they nicked a copy from the university library where they began to look for *potentials, studious girls,* though, as they both admitted, they had only read certain passages: *it was such a bloody long book.*

Nonetheless, they had read enough to develop their own Sadean system; one of the more sensational papers stated that David *forced his victims to wear white net veils embroidered with tiny white satin flowers, as if they were preparing for marriage.* In his inverted world, the honeymoon occurred prior to the nuptials; the murder and burial served as the wedding ceremony, in which he was both husband and priest and Catherine the jealous bridesmaid, never the bride.

I looked forward to waking up in the morning, so I could get the latest installment.

I had to wait for my mom to do the crossword and then for my dad to finish the paper, but the wait was worth it.

To read about horror that doesn't touch you or anyone you love; could there be anything better?

David's younger brother came out of the woodwork, claiming that David had *forcibly sodomized him multiple times,* during a lapse in the couple's relationship.

When Catherine returned, David summoned his brother into their bed, offering Catherine to him as a gift for his eighteenth birthday. *It was his way of saying sorry,* the brother said. *I figured it was alright, as they weren't really married, just de facto.*

That article's headline was "Unholy Arrangements." My eyes lingered on the terms *sodomy* and *de facto*—phrases that often appeared in crime reports. I saved this article and reread it numerous times, although this aspect of the story was extraneous to the case.

I'm still not sure what word would best encapsulate the feeling that bloomed inside me, knowing there was nothing between me and the Birnies and the night but the flywire screens on our windows with their flimsy clasps, like the clasps on old ladies' purses, purses that could be easily unfastened, screens that kept out spiders and flies but could be opened from the outside with the flick of a wrist.

My mother had her own theory concerning the Birnies' guilt, their culpability. Over the years, on our walks, we had frequently gone down the footpath with its gray corrugated asbestos fence, past the Birnies' house.

Every time, she would lower her voice, *just in case the neighbors were about*, and comment on *the dreadful state of their garden—if you could call it that, dead grass and weeds, and some rust bucket on bricks. Just look at that*, she would whisper, *what an eyesore; they're letting the whole street down.*

When the Birnies' misdeeds were revealed, my mother was not so much horrified by the proximity but smug; her suspicions were confirmed.

Well of course they did it, she said. *Just look at the state of their garden.*

The court trial went quickly. Attention was given not to the Birnies' garden as a reflection of their moral turpitude but to the couple's personal appearance. One daily wrote of *a rather nondescript, ordinary looking couple you might find running a petrol station in a country town*. David was *a weedy little man* and Catherine was *his drab, slightly buxom wife with a sour face*.

This portrayal reminded me of that nursery rhyme couple who despite their physical differences complemented each other: *Jack Sprat could eat no fat, his wife could eat no lean. And so between them both they licked the platter clean.*

The same paper recounted how the pair behaved in court, their private displays of tenderness: the patting of each other's hands, the rubbing of each other's handcuffed wrists. *There, there*, Birnie was overheard whispering to Catherine during a particularly tense moment.

After the judge delivered the verdict—four life sentences each—and the Birnies were led outside, separately, *David gave the finger to the crowd and blew Catherine a kiss.*

At school, word got around that I lived in the same suburb as the Birnies. The other boys asked me questions: *Did you know the killers? Did you ever see them do anything out of the ordinary?*

I'm sure I made up some story. Like I heard screams one night. Or I caught sight of a scared face in their bedroom window. Every time I walked past, Catherine would glare at me and David would eye me like a snake.

But no, it was nothing like that. I only encountered the Birnies once.

It was three or four years before their spree (but, as the papers said, *they had been contemplating the idea for a long time*). So that makes me about eleven or twelve.

I was walking past the house, and David was outside, working on a car. Catherine was outside too, standing on the small porch, chatting with her common-law husband. I must have seen one or both of them before. As I passed, they stopped talking and looked up.

"Hey love," Catherine said. Her hair was long, a little greasy, and her skin was pale. She clearly wasn't getting much sun. She had on light-blue terry-toweling shorts, and I saw the purple varicose veins meandering up and down her legs, just like my mother's. "Are you heading to the shops?" she asked. "Would you mind popping this in the mailbox?"

"Okay," I said. She came over and handed me an envelope.

"But it needs a stamp. Hang on," she said as she went inside.

I waited there. David was tinkering with the car. He seemed . . . engrossed in it, this mechanical thing he needed to fix. He was shirtless, wearing a pair of jeans.

I glanced at the envelope. Someone's name was on it, in what I presume was Catherine's handwriting, an uncommon blend of print and cursive. I looked at the house. Their door was open and I saw they had a fireplace in their lounge room and I felt a tinge of envy because our house didn't have one.

Catherine came back outside and gave me money for a stamp. "Keep the change," she said, "and buy something for yourself."

"I reckon he's gonna get a beer with that, love," David said, still absorbed in the car.

He laughed and so did she. "Oh no he won't, he's a good boy," Catherine said, and ruffled my hair.

Then I went to the shops, asked for the correct stamp, licked the stamp and fixed it to the envelope, bought a chocolate bar with the change, and mailed the letter to who knows where.

You would think I might have boasted about this errand, created a plot to entertain my schoolmates, but I didn't.

Up until now I've never told anyone.

Even though it was a few years earlier, I was concerned it somehow connected me to the Birnies' crimes, made me a kind of accomplice. I could end up in jail, in a cell with David. He was housed on death row in Fremantle Prison, a limestone edifice from the mid-nineteenth century, right across the street from my school, so he was still nearby, still my neighbor. He might even be able to see me and the other boys from the tiny window in his cell.

One night, some friends and I were driving around—not going any-where in particular—and before they dropped me off, we went to see the house. We parked in the driveway, turned on the headlights, and stared. It had only been a few months since the trial and there was already a For Sale sign next to the mailbox.

At first we were messing around, cracking jokes. We laughed about who would be fool enough to buy the place. Someone suggested pitching in, becoming the proud new owners, and converting the house into a museum. We could charge admission, give visitors guided tours, show them where everything went down. *It would be even better if we could get back the evidence from the cops*, we agreed, *the bed and chains and knives and stuff. We could make a bloody fortune.*

Gradually the tone became more solemn. The longer we gazed at the house, its blue exterior bleached to near-white in the car's high beams, the more it seemed to dawn on all of us that inconceivable things went on in there.

We began to talk more earnestly, albeit in a clumsy, Catholic school-boy fashion, about the women who suffered, just behind that bedroom window, *and really, what does that mean, in the scheme of things? Why does God let this happen? And how does he make the selections? Is there some kind of infinite death lottery, a huge plastic sphere full of billions of balls with black numbers, and the sphere is constantly tumbling and if your number comes up, congratulations, you'll die a violent death at the hands of some sick bastard. . . . Or does God pull names out of a big hat, like in a raffle? That must be how it works, it must be arbitrary; God wouldn't have any other criteria, would he?*

And then we stopped talking, and the longer we sat in Wayne's Camaro, just staring at the house, the more it seemed as if the house wanted to tell us . . . not so much a story, but something untellable that was trying to seep out through the cracks in the walls and the holes in the floorboards. Basically, we scared ourselves shitless, deliberating what those girls had gone through, and so we drove off to our homes and our beds.

For a bored teenage boy like myself, it was . . . thrilling, I think that's the best word to use, to be on the doorstep of this site of . . . atrocity.

Thanks to the Birnies, I was taken out of, away from, the tedium of everyday life. (Speaking of which, Birnie later claimed in an interview that he committed those acts to escape life's uniformity. *Perth is so fucking dull*, he said. *The dullest city in the world. A man can only take so much peace and quiet.*)

I managed to find a copy of *120 Days of Sodom* at a secondhand bookstore in Fremantle and would go there after school to read sections on the sly. Like David, I was enchanted, transported, yet I only got so far; it's such a long book.

For a while my sister Julianne had nightmares; this was understandable. I'd inquire about these nightmares, but she would not elaborate.

I had dreams of a different nature. Once again, I was posting that letter for the Birnies. Catherine was kind to me, motherly, ruffling my hair. David was even friendlier, calling me mate.

But this time, my errand coincided with the murders. The letter was from the girl they captured. I was the couple's messenger. The name *Susannah Candy* was written in the upper-left corner, just the name, no return address, in the girl's trembling handwriting. *Candy*, what Americans call chocolate, like what I bought with the change.

There were other dreams, dreams of David and me and his younger brother. I'd wake up sticky, disconcerted.

The dreams recurred, and then they ceased.

Inevitably, other serial killers emerged on the scene. Either they got caught, or, taking advantage of the emptiness of Western Australia, all that space, the killers folded themselves up neatly into the landscape and disappeared.

Talk of the Birnies quieted down. You would hear about them now and then. Parole cases denied, that sort of thing. Colleen Sheir, *the lucky one*, was interviewed on local TV, avowing how difficult it had been to go on with her life: *I feel as though I died with the other women. I don't feel like I'm alive. When you've been on the brink of death, seen your own death, you go on seeing it.*

Although David and Catherine would not see each other again, they wrote more than two thousand letters to one another from prison. Someone was seeking to publish the letters; I think there would still be a readership for them.

The correspondence stopped when David committed suicide, hanging himself in his cell with a nylon cord on October 6, 2005, the same date the first girl vanished nearly twenty years before. The parallel was noted.

He was buried in an unmarked pauper's grave at Pinnaroo Cemetery, not far from the forests where they disposed of the girls. No one attended the funeral except for a priest who said a few words.

Catherine's still alive, head of the library at Bandyup Women's Prison. Apparently, she takes real pride in her job.

She must have mourned David terribly. Does she continue to mourn? With no one to write to anymore, she has reportedly been working on a book of her own, a sci-fi fantasy that takes place in a kind of afterlife, though not as we conceive it, the virtuous sent to one domain, the evil sent to another. In her version, everyone's lumped together in a junkyard afterlife that is neither above nor below us. Its laws and morals have no relation to those on earth. An excerpt of her novel was even published in the prison's paper. I could not obtain a copy but the names of the two heroes are David and Catherine; the working title is *Our Dark Adventure*.

I don't remember why I used to go by the Birnies' house. There was a more direct route to the park or the deli. Perhaps for a change in scenery?

Their place on Moorhouse stayed vacant for years until a developer bought it at a knockoff price and immediately knocked it down.

The suburb of Willagee is of significance in Nyoongah mythology: it's a black-hearted zone, a zone where bad things happen and evil spirits dwell. The pine forests attracted these entities; they liked something about the shade. The forest is all gone now, cleared to make way for new houses. Where do you think evil spirits go when their shade is gone?

Brushes with Death

As you cross Slauson and make your way to the cemetery, exercise caution. Otherwise you'll end up flattened like those squirrels you see all over LA, so desiccated they resemble beef jerky with fur trimming. Continue to be alert once you're inside the grounds. Cars speed through there, like the roads are an extension of the freeway, and the cemetery is a continuation of the city, life and death forming one unceasing . . . loop. Don't let the headstones distract you; they're merely identifying symbols, like license plates.

When I was in first grade, my cousin Paul tried to crack open my skull with a cricket bat. Paul was nine years older than me, with chalk white skin and black buttery hair. He's gentle now, and his hair is gray, but his teenage years were difficult. He has this condition that I think I share, to a degree. Paul was staying over and my parents had gone out for the evening and we were having some dispute over the television. I got up and changed the channel, and he lost it. He grabbed a bat and chased me around the house, yelling that he was going to *bash my brains in.*

My brother Jamie and my sister Fiona eventually restrained Paul, but not before he broke a painting in the living room, a Parisian street scene. In the background, Sacre Coeur's dome glowed white as a skull, just as my skull might have glowed, if Paul had been successful.

Everyone calmed down and I apologized to Paul for changing the channel. Dad took the painting to the framers the next day to be repaired.

58

When I was twenty or twenty-one, I had an awful stomachache. I stayed in bed for a day or two, taking bicarbonate of soda.

But one night I woke up and knew something was wrong; it was a form of pain I had not experienced before.

A couple of friends drove me to the emergency room. I remember pressing my face up against the car window, trying to get out of the car to escape the pain. At the hospital I blacked out on the gurney. Turns out I had appendicitis. They took my appendix out right away.

"You were fortunate," the doctor said the next morning. It seems my useless organ was on the point of bursting and poisoning my bloodstream. "You almost went septic," he told me. I thought of my parents' septic tank, that underground apparatus in which sewage lingers and is processed for several days before the tank is drained. Still blissed out from the surgical drugs, I shared this thought with the doctor, who informed me that *the human septic system is far less efficient.*

This one happened here in LA, when I was living in that studio in Santa Monica.

One night I was a little lonely and I went out for a walk on Ocean Boulevard. Some old guy pulled up alongside me. He was driving one of those faux-wood station wagons from the 1970s, the kind that look like they're made out of coffins that have been dismantled then soldered back together. He attempted to convince me to come home with him.

"I have a beautiful wife," he said. "Blonde, big bosom." That's the word he used, *bosom.*

"I can pay you," he said. "I won't touch you. I'll just stand outside and watch through the window."

I've got good instincts, at least I like to think I have, and I sensed there was something dubious about this guy and his proposition. He never leaned out the window, stayed inside, but I could see he had one of those faces that are suspiciously unmemorable; if you pulled off his wire-rimmed glasses, you would tear off his features and his entire face would disappear.

"Thanks, I'm okay," I said. "I'm just heading home."

I kept walking, but he kept driving alongside me, repeating the offer, muttering, until he yelled "Get in" and opened the car door and grabbed the sleeve of my sweater with his manicured hand.

Spooked, I ran back to my dumpy studio and kept on looking back to make sure he hadn't followed. Maybe I was being paranoid, but an inner voice told me that if I was dumb enough to get in his car I would have found a soft rag stuffed in my mouth, soaked in chloroform. They never actually caught the guy who killed the boy from UCLA—*the killer continues to evade authorities*—and I had this hunch, sort of a vision, that this might have been him. (Which reminds me, it wasn't the boy's skeleton they recovered, nothing that substantial, just ash and bone fragments, mixed up with the ashes of some other dead boys in the incinerator in that basement in Oregon.)

The ceiling of my basement apartment caved in, just a few months later; I slept right through this calamity and woke up unharmed with everything covered in white dust and plaster.

There was one more recently, not at night but during the day.

Last spring I went to see the California poppies. I read an article about them in the *Los Angeles Times*.

I don't have my driver's license, did I mention that? It's just . . . well, I don't like being left alone to my own devices inside a machine. Tim was away—his work takes him out of town—so I really had to make an effort. I took a bus downtown and then rode the train to Lancaster and another bus to the Poppy Reserve.

When I finally got there, it was practically time to go home. I was walking quickly, all the orange flowers were invading my field of vision, when someone came up behind me and touched me lightly on my shoulder.

"Look," he said. Ahead of us on the dirt path was a snake, maybe six feet away. "It's a rattlesnake," he said, real quietly, as if he didn't want it to hear him, didn't want the snake to know he knew what it was.

The snake was still, lying flat on the ground. It was very pale, like it had just shed its skin and was between skins. I could see a faint diamond pattern.

"If the fucker was closer," the guy whispered, "I would cut off its head with my knife, but they can inject you with their venom for an hour after they've been beheaded. Did you know that?"

Just as we began to step back, the snake shook its rattle: it was doing this for show; the snake knew it wasn't in danger. The sound was artificial and unthreatening as a baby's rattle.

I never got a good look at the stranger. Near the reserve's entrance, I saw the rattlesnake warning sign, which I had overlooked: a yellow triangle with the word CAUTION below it in bold black caps, a curly snake inside the triangle, its tongue flickering, fangs bared, quivery lines around its tail to indicate rattling. *Reasonable watchfulness should be sufficient to avoid snakebites*, the sign read.

Those are a few times when I brushed up against death. I bet I could think of more, if I put my mind to it.

Demographics

*The relationship between the living and the dead is not fixed;
it is unstable. The relationship is not reciprocal. We are
above ground thinking about the dead who are below ground,
ignoring the living.*

The population of Holy Cross as it currently stands is 163,471. You can call the mortuary office for this figure, though the employees can be reluctant to give it.

The last time I called was a couple of weeks ago, so we can assume more people have moved in since then, to begin disintegrating.

Just a stone's throw away from the cemetery, at the entry to or exit from the 90 Freeway, depending on which direction you're coming from, there's a sign that says *Welcome to Culver City, Population 38,883.* This figure is taken from the 2010 census. At the time of the 2000 census, the population was 38,816. Population is up ever so slightly in this city that is primarily encompassed by the city of Los Angeles though also borders several unincorporated areas.

Whereas Holy Cross's residents reside in graves, niches, or crypts in either individual or collective arrangements, within its 5.1 square miles Culver City's inhabitants live primarily in condominiums and single-family houses, along with a significant number of apartment buildings and even a trailer park right next to the cemetery. I would venture that a family plot is the equivalent of a single-family house; a crypt in the mausoleum is the counterpart of a condo or a nice apartment; while a crematory niche is obviously a small studio.

This is the only statistical data I can offer in terms of the structure of these two populations, but some general conclusions can still be drawn.

Holy Cross is more densely populated than Culver City. It has a higher number of humans, if you can still call them that, per unit of area. I should probably go further into the quantifiable characteristics of the cemetery's tenants, but I'm worried if I do I might go too far.

Above ground, though there may appear to be movement, all those drivers in their automobiles twisting their necks and checking their little mirrors, their beautiful cars brushing up against one another without crashing into each other—a shining example of civilization and its collective repression of all those death-wishes—Culver City is static to the point of being stagnant. Below ground, and behind those niches, Culver City is bustling, booming, thriving. As long as there is space to inter and inurn, Holy Cross can only keep growing. People in this modest corner of LA seem to be less interested in being born and more intent on dying.

And who can blame them? Outside the metal gates, Culver City is neither picturesque nor stimulating, just buildings and billboards and freeways, glass and steel and concrete in various formations, interrupted here and there by straggly palm trees.

Inside the gated community of Holy Cross, despite the initial visual letdown, you sense there is something more vital than life teeming beneath us. Apart from the maintenance men tending the grounds in their livor-blue uniforms and the occasional stray Goth visiting Bela Lugosi, I often feel like I have the place to myself, but I'm aware this sensation of tranquility and solitude is just an illusion.

Heidi's Book

*In a magician's vanishing act, a man wearing a black cape
locks another man in an upright black box. The magician
waves his wand and intones a series of words and makes the
confined man disappear. Then he intones some more words
and waves his wand again and the guy comes back. It should
be noted that he participates of his own volition. With death, a
form of magic we're forced to undergo, we don't return, though
our corpse is still here, a locked and empty black box. I can't
decide if this makes death a more successful or less successful
act.*

Some people think you shouldn't loan books out, because you'll never
get them back.

That's what happened with me and Heidi. She used to live next
door to us, in the back unit of the fourplex.

She was already living there when Tim and I moved in to our place
in Venice, shortly after that incident involving my kitchen ceiling, in
the late summer (or was it the early fall?) of 1998.

The moving process was exhausting; the previous owner had
stripped our new house of everything, even the light fixtures, leaving
only the wires.

My knowledge of Heidi is limited to the following. She was German
and had retained an accent. She was an accountant. She liked to garden.
She was . . . in her fifties? Heidi wore glasses, with thin silver frames.

She had gray curly hair and a sharp face that might have been pretty when she was young.

She . . . the more I try to represent her, to present her likeness, the more I try to portray anyone, especially the people who've gone, the more they slip out of my grasp.

But I feel a need to keep talking; otherwise I'll just plunge into silence. And then what will we do?

Our relations with Heidi were neighborly, cordial, but distant—you don't want to get too friendly with your neighbors. All tangled up in their business.

Heidi made more of an effort; she gave us produce from her garden, basil and tomatoes and zucchinis. When she heard us in the backyard, she would say *hi* and talk to us through the slats of the fence. I could hear her but couldn't see her, or just barely. *Hang on*, she'd say, and then she would climb up on her ladder, bearing her vegetables. I can still see her on that ladder, wearing a big sun hat, her sweet, sharp face peering over.

Heidi did accounting the old-fashioned way, in hard-backed ledgers, entering the transactions by hand. She showed me one of her ledgers once. I don't know why. I must have asked to see it. She had this exceptionally neat handwriting, perfectly formed letters and numbers that were so small I'm surprised anyone could make sense of her bookkeeping.

I told her that I did accounting for a while, in high school, and at first I was pretty good at it, but soon I began to lose track of the basic principles. I would get the credit and debit columns confused, the distinction between those categories, which posed a fundamental problem to my ongoing success in the subject.

And the process began to disturb me. Somehow it seemed too . . . symbolic, of the relationship between life and death. From God's vantage point, we're all numbers, it's nothing personal, he's just balancing the books: what we thought was an asset becomes a liability; everyone's name ends up in the debit column eventually. Though doesn't debit have a positive value in double-entry bookkeeping?

Heidi nodded and laughed; I could not tell if she understood or thought I was insane.

Years went by. So many things must have happened in that time, but they're all lost or I've put them somewhere else for safekeeping.

I can say this. For a while with me and Tim it was touch and go. He didn't trust what I got up to while he was traveling. He began to tire of my impulses.

I'm glad he stuck around. I'm the kind of person who needs someone to quietly insinuate himself between me and the world, someone who'll shield me from death or life or a sinister combination of both.

One afternoon Tim and I were on the street; we had been out walking, talking things over, and Heidi was washing her car. She had a bucket of dirty, soapy water. I have no recollection of the model or color of her car but the bucket was blue, the shade old ladies dye their hair. Tim asked Heidi how her day was going, and she paused for a moment.

"Okay," she said, soft rag in hand, but her voice sounded a little funny, like something was going on and she wasn't sure if she should share it with us. For some reason known only to her, she decided to say more.

"I have to go into the hospital for a procedure tomorrow, to have my ovaries removed," she said.

Everything blurs here, but I'm sure we expressed our sympathy and asked her about her condition and wished her well.

"We'll see," she said, and went back to washing the car.

Heidi was gone for a while. Then one night, say, six weeks later, I was opening our front gate when I saw Heidi. She was wearing denim shorts and a gray camisole edged with lace. Her hair was longer. Hair can grow considerably in six weeks. She was with a young woman who turned out to be her daughter. There was no family resemblance.

"How are you?" I asked. "We've been thinking about you." This was not entirely true. In fact, I had forgotten all about her.

"Oh, better," Heidi said. "I'm just out of hospital. Though I developed a blood clot in my leg; that's why I was in so long. Complications from the surgery. They almost had to remove it. My leg, I mean. I almost died."

Heidi didn't look like someone who had approached death, someone whose innards had been thoroughly scooped out. She was smiling and a bit giddy; this may have been due to the drugs still circulating in her system. Dressed so casually, she looked like she had just returned from vacation.

"We're glad to have you back," I said. I meant that.

The smell of the night-blooming jasmine was intense, and Heidi breathed it in, practically swooned. Or maybe that was me? I wanted to question her further, but she seemed in a rush to get inside.

When people have cancer, regardless of the form, there is often a similar story, a foreseeable sequence of events.

Heidi went on chemo.

She lost her hair and her appetite. She got real skinny.

Sometimes when I was in the backyard, I would hear Heidi retching.

She and her body followed the story faithfully, word for word.

Whenever I saw Heidi I would ask how she was doing, but at some point I stopped asking; I did not want to intrude.

She continued to give us vegetables. I can still see her, standing on the ladder, in the sunlight, handing me some zucchinis and tomatoes, praising their reds and greens. The skin on her neck and arms had become gray and flaky, another side effect of the chemo, like the gray dust from an eraser left on a page.

Once, we ran into her at the theater, a night of mediocre performance art at some small airless black box in Hollywood. Heidi was foregoing wigs and her head was bald, covered in a light moon-like layer of silver stubble. She was dressed in black and looked very chic; cancer had invested her with a certain glamour. A friend we were with asked Heidi if she was a performance artist.

"No, I'm an accountant," she said.

At the time of Heidi's illness, there was a property boom in Venice—is there a link between the descent in her body and the rise in real estate values? This remains unclear, but the fourplex was sold and Heidi was kicked out. As required by law, she was given a relocation sum of six thousand dollars. She found an apartment in West LA.

"It's not as nice," she said. "Let's stay in touch."

"Of course" I said. Of course I didn't.

Before Heidi moved out, before she died of cancer of the ovaries, I loaned her a book by a German writer. I thought Heidi might like it; there was the German connection, and the main character in the novel, who was essentially the author, had a love of gardening. The story took place in the days after the Chernobyl disaster, when there was that crack in the nuclear reactor, and everyone in Europe thought it was poisoning the air and the soil. The woman in the book was unperturbed; she kept gardening, daily, compulsively.

"Have you started reading it? What do you think?" I asked Heidi one day through the slats of the fence.

"Yes, but I haven't got very far. It's quite difficult," she said.

As Heidi was packing up, I thought about asking for the book. I knew I wouldn't see her again. But I couldn't bring myself to do this. You don't ask a dying woman who is being evicted to return a book. You just don't do that.

Heidi left a box on the verge: kitchen items mostly, some bowls, cups, measuring utensils, frying pans. I rifled through them, to see if there was anything of use.

The only item I kept was at the bottom of the box: one of her ledgers. It wasn't even blank, as if she had begun keeping the books for a business and then given up. Who would want a half-filled ledger?

I guess I would. In its pages divided into two columns of fine blue lines are the financial accounts I don't understand of a business I have no stake in: meaningless calculations, transactions, numbers.

The new owner of the fourplex tore the fence down. It was rotting and termite-ridden, and besides, the property lines were incorrect, so a new fence had to be rebuilt, reducing the width of our yard by four inches. I was not happy about this. For a few days, while it was under construction, I had an unobstructed view of Heidi's old place, the gnarled remains and roots of her garden.

I spoke too soon about not seeing Heidi again. She had promised to drop in sometime when she was in the neighborhood, and although she never did, perhaps sensing we wouldn't welcome such an unexpected visit, I dreamt of her, like I dream of everyone who's dead.

Heidi came to the door, vegetables in hand. She looked better: she had more flesh on her bones, more color in her cheeks. But I wouldn't let her in, even in a dream.

"I'm busy," I said.

"That's okay," she said, though she sounded hurt.

I would not accept her vegetables. They were covered in dirt; they could be poisoned. Heidi was offended.

"You're as skinny as a lead pencil," she told me, turning to leave. "You should eat before you disappear completely."

Dreams aside, I like to think that the dead are our neighbors. Sometimes when I'm in the backyard, I try to concentrate to see if I can perceive . . . not Heidi's image but her ghost peering at me over the fence, offering me something.

Or I shut my eyes and listen, to see if I can hear her speaking, or trying to. If ghosts exist, I imagine their relationship to language is tenuous, even more tenuous than mine. Ghosts must retch up language; all their words must come out garbled.

Could be I'm not looking or listening hard enough, but I don't see or hear anything.

And if I'm being totally honest with you, if such a thing is possible, I don't feel any sadness over Heidi, not really, not in my heart where I should feel it, but I'm filled with regret about that novel I loaned her, the book Heidi borrowed from me.

What do you think happened to it?

Most likely, when she died, when Heidi was forced to move yet again—death is a form of relocation, stripping us of everything—her daughter cleaned up her apartment and sorted out her things. She would have kept some items that belonged to her mother, articles of personal value, keepsakes, but surely not that book. She probably put her mom's books in a box and took them to the local library, donated them to the *free books* section.

Either someone picked up that book and it's in their possession, or it's still out there.

From time to time, I get an overwhelming desire to go looking for that book. Wherever it is.

I can't remember the name of the book or the author, but it doesn't matter, because I only want the copy Heidi read, the one she held in her sunspotted hands.

You see, I've formed this idea that Heidi read it as she was dying and scribbled notes in the margins, an account of what she was undergoing. I write notes in every book I read, don't you?

Perhaps she didn't write much, not a story, just annotations on her own death: random, disconnected thoughts. That would be more than enough.

This notion of mine has no foundation whatsoever. But I don't care. I'm convinced that in the book, which Heidi is unable to return to me, written in her accountant's hand, is the partial story of the infinite particulars of her own disappearance.

Notable Persons

A question I've been meaning to ask you: Who died the year you were born?

In 1971, the year I was born, the following people died: Louis Armstrong, Nikita Khrushchev, Coco Chanel, Jim Morrison, Harold Lloyd, and Igor Stravinsky.

I know this because we used to get these *Year Books* chronicling everything that had gone down the year before. We kept them in sequential order, lined up next to the regular *Encyclopedia* in a cupboard in the hall. I was intrigued by the volume that recounted the events of 1971, especially the Deaths of Notable Persons section. Each dead person received one or two sentences explaining who they were.

I studied those six pages diligently; I can still quote some of the phrases. *Chanel was a designer who enjoyed being copied. Stravinsky was a man with a flair for fur-collared greatcoats. Harold Lloyd's lenseless horn-rimmed glasses were his trademark. Jim Morrison was found dead in the bathtub in his Paris apartment.*

I can still see some of the little black-and-white pictures. There was a photo of Khrushchev, pale and waxy in his open casket, surrounded by flowers and women in headscarves. A fat Jim Morrison in Paris, dressed in funereal black leather. *World War II hero* Audie Murphy, saluting, his uniform weighed down by his *twenty-four medals*, years before *the Texas farm boy went bankrupt and was found dead in the wreckage of his private plane.*

There were other less notable people in the list with whom I became acquainted. Like Edna Ballard, leader of some kooky religious movement that didn't believe in death. And Nathan Leopold, who with his accomplice Richard Loeb murdered a fourteen-year-old boy named Bobby Franks in Chicago in 1924 (the same year Armstrong *with his ever-present white handkerchief* made his first jazz recording in the Windy City).

Then there were people whose names I can no longer recall: the actor who did the voices for Sleepy and Grumpy in *Snow White and the Seven Dwarfs*; the man who was the voice of Jiminy Cricket in *Pinocchio*; a *highly respected* German historian who translated some Babylonian clay tablets that *illuminated a code of laws* from the nineteenth-century BC, thousands of years before the idea of Jesus Christ even existed; the guy who invented parking meters; the inventor of Yo-Yos; the founder of J. C. Penney's; and, I almost forgot, these three Russian cosmonauts who, after orbiting the earth for twenty-four days and conducting numerous experiments on one another, landed safely, or so everyone thought, in their space capsule, which I want to say was called *Dostoevsky*, but when the lid of the spacecraft was opened, all three were dead, yet physically intact, something to do with decompression and *a major seal failure*.

More than anything, it would be pitiful to die and be nameless, like all the people who ended up in the Disasters section of the *Year Book*: the forty-five vets who perished in their beds at the VA hospital in Sylmar during the '71 earthquake *which jarred the Los Angeles area*; the thirteen wedding guests in a village in France, who, when the floor of the hall collapsed during the reception, *fell into an ancient well and drowned in its waters*—not even the village's mayor who committed suicide the next day by leaping into the well earned a personal mention; or the assorted number of passengers strapped into their seats on Bulgarian and Peruvian and Libyan airliners that crashed in *dense fog, dense jungle, a sandstorm*, all of whom died as anonymous and faceless as their flight numbers.

I fantasized that one day I would be included in those preceding six pages that were far more illustrious—perhaps I would also be found dead in the bathtub of my Paris apartment. Then the question would be reversed and become more difficult to answer: *Who was born the year that you died?*

It was like I was . . . hypnotized by that list. (Or did the book's mildewy odor make me a little high, sending me into a minor trance?) There were so many variables determining the rate of vanishing. I hoped that all the entries combined would reveal something extraordinary, illuminate some ancient code of laws. Unfortunately, I never came up with anything more meaningful than the observation—the suspicion— that the terms *eminent* and *obscure* are as interchangeable as the terms *life* and *death.*

Even so, I liked knowing who had exited the world the same time I entered the world. It seemed that people were entering and exiting constantly, simultaneously.

The Mourners

The word mourn *is a verb. Contrary to what our teachers told us, a verb is not just a doing word. A verb also conveys a mode of being.* To mourn *is not merely when you feel and show intense sorrow over someone's death, the disappearance of someone, but when you feel and do not show that sorrow. Instead you reside in* an unseen state of undoing.

It would be good if we could time our visit to Holy Cross when there's a funeral in progress. This would provide us with a visual element.

I've only happened to be there once when a service was taking place. At first I couldn't see it. I heard some music playing, austere, delicate but discordant, so I began walking in that direction.

After walking awhile I saw the funeral, on the other side of the hill: a crowd of people wearing black clothes—this is a long-held social convention. The mourners were so tiny from far away, like black specks, sad insects. The hearse looked like a toy. There was smog in the air that day and the scene was smudgy at the edges; it reminded me of that unfinished painting of Baudelaire's funeral, which hardly anyone attended, apparently, because most of his friends were away on holiday and Paris was so hot!

As I made my way toward the mourners, the music stopped. A recording; there was no sign of an orchestra. Feeling somewhat exposed, I stood behind a scrawny tree. I could make out a black speck with a dash of violet and red that I presumed was the priest. I could not hear his homily, but I figured he was talking of dust and valleys and shadows of death. I wondered if his words were providing solace or if the mourners

75

collectively refused to be consoled. Though surely there would be vast degrees of feeling between those in attendance. Some of the mourners are unbearably sad, I thought, while others are mildly upset, and others aren't sad at all.

Slowly, a black shiny rectangle emerged from the hearse: the coffin. There was a black shimmering in the air: the coffin was moving, supported by four black vertical shapes that I deduced were men in suits. Some of these men would have needed to rent their suits. I left my threadbare hiding spot. I wanted to see the coffin being lowered into the ground; I've never seen that.

I did not want to be accused of showing disrespect, so I could not get near enough to see the coffin properly—the lowering—but I became aware of a thin black vertical shape topped off with a broad black horizontal sphere that I reasoned was a woman wearing a hat. She must be the widow of the man being buried, I thought. Widows wear large hats. The widow shape began to shake, she must be weeping, I thought, and she followed the shimmering as it began to . . . descend and then she and her shape went horizontal; she must be bending down to throw some dirt on her husband's coffin, I thought. I caught a flash of something very white; I inferred she had taken off one of her gloves.

The black widow shape became vertical again, and I was about to edge in even closer, so I could see the look on her face, which might have disclosed what she was truly feeling, or perhaps denied it, but then I heard a cry on the wind and the sphere flew off her head and began tumbling toward me, like an abstract tumbleweed. She called out to me to grab it, but I acted like I didn't hear. As my grandma said, it's bad luck to touch a widow's hat.

And I began walking in the opposite direction.

The Dancing Corpse of Jill Yip

A corpse is a dead body, usually human. Though in Middle English it just meant body, *human or animal, alive or dead.*

I've only laid eyes on one corpse. The corpse of Jill Yip. Jill was a dancer. A dancer is someone whose body moves.

Jill's body stopped working. She died from an intestinal obstruction. This is when an abnormality blocks the intestines and the digestive system stops functioning and then everything breaks down. You can see X-rays of this condition on the Internet. There is a soft and hazy quality to the images: the bones, the dilated loops of bowel, the obstructions in question.

From what I heard, Jill had been experiencing pain, cramps, spasms. She thought the pain would pass. She went to the emergency room, near her apartment in Alhambra. They didn't x-ray her. They must have been busy that night. They looked her over and gave her some pills and then sent her back home.

I imagine Jill tried to get some sleep. The pain woke her up; it will pass, it always does. But this was a new form of pain and she sensed something was wrong as her body went . . . haywire.

I believe Jill's roommate was out at the time but was the one who later discovered her corpse.

There was some speculation that the harsh discipline of dancing had led to Jill's death. One of the definitions of dance is *to bring to a particular state or condition by dancing; e.g., she danced herself to exhaustion.*

Dancing is hard on bodies and on the internal organs. Dance forces the body to do things it isn't necessarily designed to do.

I'm increasingly aware that death forces language to do things it was not designed to do. Language breaks down; it experiences cramps, spasms.

I saw Jill dance a handful of times. She danced with a company, but once I saw her perform a solo. Her only solo. I think it was called *Pirate Dance*. It was one of those dances with talking; Jill talked as she, her body, moved. She told a story about her past. A story is a series of sentences that move.

When Jill was a small girl, her family fled Vietnam on a boat. The journey was long and arduous. Pirates came on board and raped the women and children, threw some men overboard, left them to drown or to be eaten by sharks. Jill had to drink seawater. You could tell she was leaving all sorts of things out.

For the performance, Jill wore a pirate's hat made out of newspaper. She wore a black eye patch, a belt around her waist, with a silver plastic pirate's knife in a gold plastic scabbard: a child's Halloween costume. She said the men who came on board wore fake paper hats, *like they were pretending to be pirates, but that everything they did was real.*

Jill and her family survived the journey and reached America.

At school, Jill said, wielding her fake knife at members of the audience, *when my teacher asked me what I wanted to be when I grew up, I told her I want to be a pirate.*

The dance ended with Jill intoning these lines again and again: *I want to be a pirate. I want to commit atrocities. I did not succumb to the pirates. I escaped them.*

I have no memory of the actual dance, the steps, the gestures, and even if I did, I would be unable to explain it to you, because it's my belief, a belief that borders on the category of the spiritual, that the body moves outside of language.

There was no music, I can say that. Sometimes Jill would stop talking and dance silently, with a delicate and controlled violence. She would start to talk about what happened to her on that ship, but her words would sort of . . . drift off, and she would replace them with the ragged sound of her breathing and the clomping sound made by her feet.

When I learned of Jill's death—Tim told me, one of the other dancers in her company had called him, he came into the kitchen to convey the news—it struck me as very . . . unjust.

What bothered me was not that Jill was twenty-nine, a month or two older than me, not even the hospital's oversight, but the manner of death. Jill had overcome all those dangers as a child, made herself sick from salt water, come all this way, only to die . . . like this.

Somehow, I thought, staring at our kitchen walls, which are a bright Mexican blue, it would have been better to die at the hands of those pirates.

Jill's cool, clipped voice ran through my head: *I did not succumb to the pirates. I escaped them.*

Jill Yip's corpse was situated in a funeral parlor in Alhambra. Tim and I drove out there with our friends Danielle and Tre. Danielle's a redhead; Tre has jet black hair. Though apart from Jill, who cares what any of us look like.

We all dressed in dark colors. The car was cramped and the day was warm and dusty.

The funeral parlor was on a street lined with factories—bed manu-facturers, primarily—and other funeral parlors. A funeral parlor is a kind of factory; it makes death on a mass scale, through a process of maintaining. A parlor with a crematorium is also a factory, one that doesn't produce anything but destroys things.

Yet reducing a body down to an urnful of ash—you're still making something.

When we arrived at the parlor, the foyer was filled with people, mostly Jill's young dancer friends, who were also dressed in dark colors. There were all these photos of Jill, prints of various sizes, pinned to the walls.

Like death, or dancing, beauty cannot be described, but the photos provided evidence that Jill was small and pale with dark hair and eyes so dark I would call them black. She was fine-boned. She had amazing cheekbones, like God had stuck those compasses that are used to draw circles and arcs in geometry beneath her skin. Hers was an exquisite, severe form of beauty.

I was about to say the event in Alhambra was a funeral, but it wasn't. This was a viewing. I've never been to a funeral, but as I understand it, that event is a formal affair; there are eulogies and choreographed actions and the body is positioned in its final resting place.

A viewing is an informal affair; its main purpose is to perceive the body.

There are no eulogies, which, in my opinion, is preferable. Language only obstructs our ability to see death.

Without words, it gives us a chance to have a more . . . immediate relationship to the corpse.

We sat down for a while in the chapel on hard wooden pews and then Tim got up to view the body.

As he walked down the aisle toward Jill, her corpse, he made a distressing sound.

He began wailing at the sight of his student. Tim rarely shows his emotions, but when he does, they spill out violently. It's as if he becomes someone else. I'm the same; that could be why we get on.

I didn't know what to do so I sat there as Danielle went up to comfort him. He wept into her red hair. His grief, or its demonstration, was so extreme, localized in his body yet immense, it was like watching a twister, from a distance I had wrongly assumed was safe. I thought this grief might destroy him and Danielle and me; it might flatten everyone in its wake.

His emotions appeared suddenly, as if out of nowhere, then disappeared just as quickly.

When it was my turn, I went up and got as close as I could to Jill, her corpse, without touching her.

She wasn't in an open casket. Her body was wrapped in a rumpled gray cloth. There were oranges placed around her, flowers, burning incense.

I looked at the corpse of Jill Yip. I gazed upon her.

In Christian settings, it is strongly recommended that the body on view be embalmed and that the cosmetic services of a mortician are used. The goal is to create a lifelike representation of the dead, by draining the corpse of its blood and injecting the veins with chemicals as well as erasing any sign of sickness or violence, in an attempt to make the deceased look healthier and more presentable than when they were alive.

Jill's family is Buddhist and did not observe these recommendations.

Jill's skin was paler than usual and slightly blue gray. I knew there were parts of her body beneath the gray cloth that would be more purply and red, thanks to livor mortis, the fourth stage of death, when *the destruction of blood cells creates discoloration in lower or dependent body areas*, a stage she would have already gone through. There was no odor; perhaps it was masked by the sweet scent of the oranges, incense, and flowers.

She still resembled . . . herself. Though unpainted, unadorned, she reminded me, paradoxically, of a high school kid who has the role of an old person in a play, that stage makeup they wear that looks so tacky.

There was something unconvincing about Jill's corpse. She . . . it . . . seemed fake. I didn't quite believe her in the role she was playing.

Jill's death would ultimately be classified as *death by natural causes*, in that it was due to *an internal malfunction of the body not directly influenced by external forces*. Yet her corpse reaffirmed an opinion I still hold, that the distinction between *natural* and *unnatural death*—the latter including deaths as eclectic as *homicide, suicide, accidents*, and the intriguingly named *death by misadventure*—is dubious, false: all forms of death strike me as unnatural, artificial.

She seemed to have been drained of an element more essential than blood, that immaterial component we call the soul.

However, there was a trace of life. I felt like I was staring into the mouth of a volcano that wasn't extinct, merely dormant.

I would not have been shocked if Jill sat up and stood up and danced.

What's interesting is that we're meant to be terrified of the very idea of a reanimated corpse, and by the many varieties of the undead—beings who, although deceased, thanks to supernatural or demonic forces are capable of movement and in some instances of speech—at the very least, they can moan.

But I'm confident I would not have been the only one happy to see Jill rise up and dance. Even if we were alarmed by the sight of someone we thought was dead behaving as if she were alive.

I guess what I'm trying to say is we long for what would also horrify us.

Jill's corpse did not move an inch. She was so still. That's what struck me the most. Her stillness. And her silence.

Jill was exhibiting rigor mortis, the stiffness of death, quite literally: *rigor* (stiffness) *mortis* (of death). If I remember correctly from my book report, this stiffening of the limbs and joints is caused by the death of the cells in the muscles that move the skeleton, including the tongue, which is also a muscle, making speech and motion impossible.

A corpse is a body that does not move and does not speak.

A corpse is a body that does not see. Jill's eyes were closed so she did not, could not, return my gaze. Obviously, even if her eyes were open she would have been unable to: the dead's eyes no longer work; they're incapable of receiving images or recognizing light, of sending messages to the brain.

We shut their eyelids manually, with the same glue that is used for false eyelashes; this is considered a mark of respect, like drawing the shades in a house where someone has died. Then we look upon the dead, without their permission; we surreptitiously observe them as they are otherwise . . . engaged in a private activity. All mourners are no better than voyeurs, a bunch of perverts.

So we force the dead's eyes shut, not because they cannot see us but because we're concerned their eyes are accepting images from . . . elsewhere and they *can* see us when they stare at us in a fixed yet unspecified direction.

Jill's eyelids were thin and patterned, like lace curtains. Was she still seeing something? My thoughts . . . went haywire.

Finally, I broke the ice and spoke to Jill's corpse. I spoke silently. As if she could hear me.

I won't tell you what I said; that's a personal conversation.

Her lips were not quite closed, just like mine, and I may have been imagining it, but I thought I smelled her breath, or lack thereof. Like mulch deep in a forest. I wondered if there were stray words caught in her mouth, things she didn't get a chance to say, decomposing along with the rest of her. I swear I heard a whistly, echoey sound from inside her body slip through the crack in her lips.

I spoke to God as well. I'm not sure God exists; he could be a fiction, like the undead, but I converse with him regularly. It's a habit I acquired in childhood and am yet to shake.

I asked God to look after Jill, to keep her safe.

My back was turned to everyone else in the chapel, so no one, except for maybe Jill or God, could see my expression.

There I was, talking to God and a corpse, talking to two voids.

Tre went last, then we all lingered in the lobby. We did not discuss our time with Jill. I don't know how long I spent with her, a couple of minutes? It's hard to say, because a corpse is outside of time.

Actually, that's wrong. Although the dead are no longer subject to time—they're on their own time, death standard time—finite duration continues to work its bad magic on a corpse, whittling it down from something recognizable to something grisly to something that is, in the end, relatively elegant. A corpse is both inside and outside of time.

In their dark clothes, huddled in small groups, like on a playground, Jill's friends seemed very . . . self-aware; they knew they all had a role to play. Tim and I spoke to the roommate, the one who discovered the corpse, and as she spoke I searched her face to see if it revealed anything. Her face was not forthcoming. There were so many questions I wanted to ask her, but I bit my tongue.

While Tim chatted with his colleagues, I eyed one of Jill's handsome dancer friends who had these plush red lips and appeared to be completely devastated. He was standing in a group nearby; they were conferring together, softly, but feverishly.

I began to eavesdrop.

They were talking about Jill and her dreams.

It seems Jill had a recurring nightmare. Ever since she was a little girl back in Vietnam, *she had dreamt she was in a forest and was being strangled by trees.* She had the dream once or twice a year. She drew pictures of this dream in her journal; since her death, the book was being passed around. In her drawings, *the trees looked like tangled internal organs, strangulated bowels.*

Jill dreamt of her own death, someone was saying. Everyone agreed. The guy with the lips nodded, then caught my eye.

For all we know, a corpse could be a body that continues to dream but refuses to tell us these dreams, and gives no indication that it is dreaming.

Jill's friend held then broke my gaze. He went to the restroom next to the chapel, and I followed him. Normally I'm clumsy with flirting; I don't pick up on signals and make the procedure more circuitous than it needs to be, but on this occasion I acted with unusual ease. He was waiting for me in a stall, its red door cracked open, and I locked the door behind me and we coupled quickly and with a certain intensity, which was partly due to the circumstances—that is, there was a corpse a few feet away from us on the other side of the wall.

They say that life and death can be regarded as a process where the hormones build to a point, then gradually decline, until just before death, when a swell of hormones, a constellation of the weird secreted things, which I envision as miniscule black stars swirling through the bloodstream, suddenly and violently surge through the body of the dying man and . . . explode as he is *urged on* into an a-hormonal nothingness. When I closed my eyes in that bathroom stall, for a moment I could see those little black stars.

And it occurs to me now—it did not occur to me then—that we got the equation wrong, I mean in terms of sex and death. Maybe it's sex that's huge and death that's small; maybe death will bring only a miniature oblivion, a modest shattering of the self compared to the mindblowing, self-dissolving oblivion offered by a regular orgasm.

I hope I haven't said too much, though I feel as if I have. You're looking at me in such a curious way. I've heard such behavior at death-related rituals is quite common. I hope I haven't misconstrued your silence for an ease between us that isn't ease at all.

As Tim and I and the others left, we passed a large black-and-white photo of Jill that was on an easel next to the door. I took in the image, or attempted to. The image captured something of her . . . essence? She was laughing, but also stern, skeptical, as if she were saying: *All these photos obscure who I am. They have nothing to do with me. Destroy them.*

Afterward, we went to an Italian restaurant in Los Feliz. Tim ordered lasagna; Tre had spaghetti Carbonara with several kinds of mushrooms; Danielle and I both had seafood pasta, though she ordered hers without scallops. I asked her why.

They're bottom feeders, she said. *They eat the garbage of the ocean.*

As I ate, I thought about how the dead can't eat, not because they don't want to but because they can no longer digest; it was an obvious notion, but it filled me with dread.

As does this thought: when we have lost our capacity to break food down into substances that can be absorbed into the body, and the body begins to digest itself, it's time for us to be absorbed back into the world, which digests us, then shits us out, into the soft and hazy depths of the underworld.

We toasted Jill, finished our meals, then we all went back to the repetition of our everyday lives.

Jill has moved on to the repetition of death. Dying is simply exchanging one form of repetition for another. Her death was . . . untimely.

A slim obituary came out in a weekly paper, consisting of 106 words, I've checked. That's the only thing about her on the Internet. No images. Which is as it should be. As if Jill were saying: *There is no death image. Death is the obliteration of all images.*

Nowadays there would be all sorts of online tributes, anecdotes and snapshots and marginalia about Jill, floating around in cyberspace, like electronic ash. But Jill died a little too early—the summer of 2001. Not long after Mike and not long before those two planes crashed intentionally into the Twin Towers—right before we started documenting every single useless thing.

And before she left her mark. *Jill was just coming into her own as a dancer.* That's what it said in the obituary. I think the word they used was *electrifying.* This was not hyperbole. Jill shone that night she did her pirate dance, but it's better not to shine so bright. That makes it way too easy for death to find you. Safer to give off a dull steady glow.

In private, before our entanglement dissolved into nothing, that guy from the viewing told me Jill's roommate had gone up to the Zen monastery at Mount Baldy. She needed to get away. It was not clear if she was coming back.

As we lay in bed he told me about a dream of his. He was at the funeral parlor, looking for me. *You weren't there,* he said. He wandered into the restroom and even though the room was dark, he could see Jill in the corner; her corpse was giving off its own light.

If I want to go against Jill's wishes and perceive her image, all I have to do is sneak into Tim's office. He has an old smoking cabinet, which functions as an altar. Its shelves are cluttered with icons to the dead, his dead, who are not mine to talk about. There's a four-by-four photo of Jill on the top shelf, a reduced version of the one at the viewing. I look at it every time I go in there. I stare at that photograph of Jill, which like all photos is lifeless, no better than a corpse, drained of all substance.

I never shared with Tim what I did when I slipped away at the viewing. How could I explain that instead of comforting him, I seduced one of his grieving students, who, during the course of our passion, blacked out for a second when I inadvertently knocked the guy's head against the restroom's marble wall. The young man didn't seem to mind, and nor did I.

Though it's possible I'm focused on the wrong behavior. The indiscretions, Tim might understand. But if he knew the dark thread of my thoughts, not just about Jill but about everyone, how much time I spend at the cemetery, would he want to be with me? Would anyone want to even speak with me, if they knew?

Seeing a corpse, even once, has allowed me, over time, to come to these conclusions:

A corpse is the most substantial yet the most abstract thing in the world.

A corpse is a kind of receipt, confirming that a product has been paid for, a product has been received. A corpse makes it clear that a transaction has occurred.

A corpse is pure matter, more matter than we can deal with, more matter than we know what to do with.

In that it is both on view yet receding from view, a corpse is a quiet optical illusion.

But what of Jill Yip, whose corpse is a fact that outshines all the facts I have heaped upon it. Whose corpse, I must stress, did not get up and dance that day in Alhambra. I don't want to mislead you.

If I had hung around, waited for everyone to leave, once the doors of the parlor were locked, she might have put on a show. Rigor mortis only lasts for a day or two. The limbs loosen up and the dead revert to the serene state of secondary flaccidity, where the muscles relax until a corpse has the grace of a jellyfish.

Or perhaps as I watched her, as Jill lay there in her gray shroud, suspended between death and rebirth, she *was* dancing, with all those ferocious dakinis of manifold classes from *The Book of the Dead*, the sky dancers who carry parasols sewn from human skin, burn incense derived from human flesh, and wear necklaces of intestines snatched from unburnt corpses; those celestial beings who play trumpets fashioned from thigh bones and drums stretched taut on the skulls of boys, creating a music so intense they say it can split open a man's head.

According to different strands of Buddhist theology, reincarnation takes anywhere between one second and seven years after death. Jill must have been reborn by now. I'm inclined to think she came back as a dancer; she's condemned to die and return as a dancer, again and again, until her feet are ruined, her ankles shattered, until she has perfected her technique and fulfilled her promise.

A Hole in the World

A corpse could never squeeze through such a hole.

Correct me if I'm wrong, but we enter the world through a hole.

If we wish to gain access to existence, we have to push through our mother's sex, or slip through a horizontal slit cut in her belly.

What's weird is that when we leave the world, when God pushes us out of the world, there is no hole.

There's a clearly marked entrance, but not a discernible exit.

Though maybe we haven't been looking hard enough and there's a hole we all go through when we die.

This hole might be infinite, or at least capacious. Its dimensions could be similar to a regular manhole you see in the street, its edges slick and stained with souls. But I think it must be very small, this hole in the world, which would explain why we've overlooked it.

It's probably the size of a keyhole. If we found this hole, we could all line up and take turns peering through it, to catch a glimpse of death, to see what the dead get up to.

Perhaps it's more like the aperture in a microscope or a kaleidoscope. When you put your eye up to the hole, you will be able to examine the minute, whirling facets of death, death's shifting black patterns; not death itself, but its prismatic reflection.

Or is it an opening whose circumference is too narrow for us to see anything? A hole as impenetrable as a period that puts death to a sentence, tiny and foul as a hummingbird's asshole. Look all you want, the eye won't fit in this death hole; it refuses the eye.

Disintegration

Repeat after me: pallor mortis, algor mortis, rigor mortis,
livor mortis, putrefaction, decomposition, skeletonization —
this is what awaits us.

When I'm at Holy Cross, I like to sit on my bench and think about disintegration. I like to think about all the people disintegrating beneath me and around me, all the coffins full of bones and clothing and watches that have stopped ticking.

I'm not a technical person, I may have told you that already, but I make an effort when I want to understand.

As far as I can tell, there are five stages to the biological process of decomposition: bloat, fresh decay, active decay, advanced decay, and dry/remains.

On the Internet there's a sequence of photographs of a pig undergoing these five stages in a pastoral setting. In the first image the pig is pink as marzipan, but soon it becomes gray mush, and by the last image it's a small heap of black ash. Although there is something undeniably poetic about the terminology of death, the snapshots elicit the observation that when it comes to the empirical process, virtually every last trace of poetry will flee the scene.

It seems that how quickly you disintegrate depends on the kind of soil you're buried in, whether it's of *neutral acidity* or *acid peaty soil*—I believe the body deteriorates more gradually in the latter, though I have no idea about the quality of soil in Culver City. Being in a coffin slows things down, but generally you're a skeleton within a year. That is to say, you are *a framework, a supporting structure, a dried-up thing.*

91

Everyone goes through the five stages—unless you divert or speed up the process, unless you're Saint Bernadette, who, when they exhumed her corpse forty years after her death from tuberculosis in the bone of her right knee, had decided not to decompose. Yet each corpse that is open to corruption decays at its own pace, its own speed, disintegrates at its own rate, according to its own internal rhythm: at Holy Cross, there are 163,471 humans in 163,471 subtly varying states of disintegration, none of them identical, all of them unique. You and I, we'll break down into our component elements in our own special way.

Erin's Trip

The dead are disfigured by language, yet gleaming through it.

Perth to Sydney. Sydney to Los Angeles. Los Angeles to Tijuana. Tijuana to . . .

When I was a kid, my mom's friend Mrs. O'Kane used to come over some afternoons. Ann O'Kane was Irish and wore glasses with thick lenses. She's what my mother would call a character. *She was already experiencing cognitive problems*, though we did not know this at the time. Mrs. O'Kane had four daughters: Siobhan, Leah, Caitlin, and Erin.

Then one of the daughters died. You knew that, right? The dead are . . . irretrievable. I expect you knew that too. But I want to try to retrieve Erin for you.

Erin often came with her mother, who picked her up after school. She was the youngest of the girls, though a year or two older than me. The three elder daughters all had red hair and were deeply freckled, but Erin had dirty-blonde hair that was slightly unkempt, a snub nose, and brown skin with patches of sunburn.

While our mothers sat in the kitchen and drank tea and gossiped, Erin and I would go into the lounge room and lie on the carpet and watch TV. Reruns of *Looney Tunes*, *Tom and Jerry*. Those old cartoons were bright and jazzy, and above all, they were violent.

We would watch, riveted, as these cute fluffy creatures were flattened with huge frying pans, run over by trains or trucks, blown to bits by

93

cherry-red sticks of dynamite, and shattered by cannonballs; we would regard the screen in silence as these adorable yet malevolent characters fell from great heights and were smashed to pieces on the rocks or sidewalk below, or found themselves riddled with so many bullet holes that rain poured through their furred or feathered skin like a sieve; we would laugh as the critters drank poison from bottles on which the skull and crossbones had been slyly scratched out, so that their feet turned a shade of soda-pop orange that rapidly made its way up their little bodies 'til flames fizzed out of their pointy or floppy ears.

During the commercials, Erin and I would assess each other's sunburn, pull long strips of skin off each other's shoulders, hold the strips up to the light. We believed that if we kept peeling, we would uncover the skeletons crouching beneath us, just as if you dug a hole that was deep enough, you would end up in China.

Other days we would play outside. The backyard was ideal for children, overgrown and ragged and full of mysteries.

There was a charred tree we liked to climb; its trunk was wide and oddly shaped, with ledges you could perch on, like a weird wooden mountain, and in our games that's exactly what it was, the Alps, the Andes, the Himalayas.

We climbed the living trees as well, a pine tree, several gum trees, and a jacaranda; its purple blossoms would stick in our hair. We ate plums from the plum tree and rubbed the juice from the plums on the warts that occasionally appeared on our fingers or knees, an old wives' remedy.

And our rusty hulk of a barbecue served as a set on a stage. Reenacting Hansel and Gretel, we would take turns being the witch and try to push each other in.

I no longer have access to these games, their rules, their laws.

I can almost see us playing—Erin's barefoot, wearing her green Santa Maria tunic. I'm in my gray school shorts and gray short-sleeved cotton shirt—but no matter how high I turn up the volume, I cannot hear what we said to one another.

(By the way, Erin was deaf in one ear; one of her red-haired sisters stuck a Q-tip in too deep and it punctured her eardrum.)

It's as if both Erin and I created a new game, whose sole purpose was to keep things from you and from me.

Those afternoons are crudely stitched together; not much stands out, apart from one afternoon when Erin and I looked at a *Playboy* magazine.

By then we must have been twelve and ten, respectively.

Erin brought it over—she had nicked it from her dad's stash. Her father *was already exhibiting violent tendencies*, though we did not know this at the time.

We hid behind some shrubs and studied the pictures. With their enormous breasts and asses and thighs, the women were like giants: voluptuous, obscene. As the sunlight filtered in through the leaves, I stared at the magnetic space between the women's legs, with no sense that I had come from such an opening.

I observed that the images formed stories. There was one spread that began with a woman being stripped in a restaurant kitchen by a group of chefs, men wearing checked pants, white jackets and aprons, white puffy hats. After some fondling, the chefs pushed her into an industrial-sized oven. At the end of the story, she was laying on a wooden table, slathered in whipped cream, like a cream puff, portions of her body strategically bare. The chefs stood above her with knives and forks, grinning. The caption: *Good Enough to Eat.*

When we were finished with the images, or the images were finished with us, we put the porno down and examined each other's bodies, half in darkness, half in light: a mode of exploration that seemed a natural progression from the inspection of our sunburn.

I wish I could say that our mothers came outside and caught us, mouths agape. *Our mothers were appalled and we never saw each other again.*

All I can offer is that these afternoon visits dwindled away. Erin and I grew up, and apart—our minor age difference took on greater import. She stopped coming over. We withdrew from childhood at a separate pace and developed our own interests, too fragile to articulate, too nebulous to share with anyone.

Perth to Brisbane. Brisbane to Honolulu. Honolulu to San Diego. San Diego to Tijuana. Tijuana to . . .

One night, around two years ago, I was talking to my mother on the phone. I call her every fortnight on a Sunday evening. I asked her what had been going on, and she got quiet for a moment and then she said to me, "Do you remember Erin O'Kane?"

I had not seen Erin in more than twenty-five years. I hadn't thought of her either. I had kind of . . . erased her. Memory, or at least my memory, is a device inside of me that erases memories. Either my device is faulty or nothing gets erased permanently.

I told Mum of course I remembered Erin.

"Well," she said, her voice rising out of the quiet, "I'm afraid I have some sad news. Erin died, she . . . killed herself."

My mother's breathing was shallow. I gave her time to catch her breath. Then she told me Erin's story, in chronological order.

I'm the world's worst listener, except when the subject is death and my ears prick up.

It seems Erin had been depressed for some time, possibly her entire life, but had managed to make a go of it. She found herself a nice husband and they raised three lovely kids. Although she and her husband were separated, they'd recently had their fourth child. This had been hard on Erin; hit with postpartum depression, she'd been involuntarily admitted with her newborn girl to the Mother Baby Unit at Fremantle Hospital, two floors above the ward where she had just given birth. *The walls of the ward are painted orange and, oddly enough, blue,* my mother told me, *to help lift the patients' spirits.*

After several weeks, the hospital discharged Erin and she left the new baby with her husband and the other kids, telling him that *she was going down south* for a few days, *she needed to gather herself, needed a little peace and quiet.*

Instead of driving to Margaret River, a popular resort town a couple hours south of Perth—I hear it's beautiful, though I've never been— Erin headed to the airport. She boarded a plane to Tokyo. But she didn't stop there. Next, she took a flight to San Francisco, then on to Mexico City and back to Tijuana—so, in a sense, she wasn't lying, she did go down south, to Mexico, where, she had heard, you could easily buy this drug, Nembutal, a barbiturate veterinarians use, to put animals to sleep. Erin had read that it was the best drug to take if you wanted to commit suicide; it made for a gentle death. She bought a bottle at a store.

It took them a few days, but Erin's sisters realized something was up. At her flat they found printouts of various travel itineraries, comparing routes and prices to Tijuana, tucked into a book on euthanasia. Siobhan and Caitlin flew all the way to Tijuana themselves—by way of Sydney, and Los Angeles, I believe—and tracked Erin down. She was still alive, but barely, in a coma in a room in a rundown hospital. Erin died four days later.

It's just so awful," my mom said when she finished. "The husband is so lovely and now he's left with those kiddies and the baby. Poor Ann is devastated. You two were quite friendly when you were children. It must be upsetting to hear this."

"Yes," I said. I have no trouble lying to my mother, but it's more difficult lying to you. You can see right through me.

I think I was . . . surprised that someone from so long ago could reappear in such a manner, through disappearing, just like that.

After I got off the phone, I jotted down some notes. I thought about what Mom said, that *Erin may have been depressed ever since she was a young girl.* I willed myself to go back to that time, to summon more memories of Erin, to see if I could locate any signs, but I couldn't.

You know what came to mind? Those dumb cartoons we watched. In every episode, one of those chirpy animals was mortally wounded, yet they would laugh it off, take a dip in a cooling body of water to extinguish the fire that had burned them to a crisp, brush off the black gunpowder with their wings or paws or claws, unflatten or dehole themselves, cheerfully reassemble their severed limbs and appendages, and get back to the chase.

No one—Tom, Jerry, Sylvester, Tweetie-Bird, Coyote, or Road-Runner—ever truly died. Whether the character was sympathetic or diabolical—like most children I rooted for the so-called villains, though good and evil is complicated in the *Looney Tunes* and cannot be taken at face value—they all knew how to outwit death. No matter how extreme the incident, how pulverized they were, how torn apart, each technicolor creature would return from the dead; the cute little guys would die and be reborn over and over again in an endless bright loop of violence.

Everything else in my head was a blur, and so was Erin. Death . . . smudges us. Sometimes death makes people clearer, sharpens their outlines, but not Erin. She was more indefinite than ever.

Turns out I didn't need to write any of it down because there was so much about her in the papers back home; it was all over the news. One of the tabloids printed a photograph from the wedding day of one of Erin's sisters. The wedding party is dressed as you would expect: white for the bride, tuxes for the groom and best man, pastels for the bridesmaids and matrons of honor. Everyone appears to be delighted, exuberant.

But there's a woman standing off to the side, dressed in black, some vintage frock from the 1940s by the look of it; she's wearing a black pillbox hat and black net veil that conceals her face. Erin looks out of place yet stylish, nothing like the straggly girl I remembered. I couldn't make out her expression through the dense black veil.

Naturally, the papers stretched the truth, misrepresented the facts, until it was hard to tell what was a fact and what was embellished:

They said that *39-year-old Erin Jansen purchased the 100 ml emerald green bottle of Nembutal hidden in the garish papier-mâché belly of a piñata—the drug was routinely smuggled across the U.S. border in this manner. The smashed remnants of the piñata and the candy crammed inside were scattered on the floor of her hotel room, near her comatose body.*

Every article referred to the book her sisters found in her flat, a book by a Dr. Philip Nitschke, *a vocal advocate for voluntary euthanasia and the rights of the terminally ill.* (When my mother mentioned this, I thought she said that Erin had been reading a book by Nietzsche.)

Erin's copy—*borrowed from her local library and severely overdue*—was full of Post-its, apparently, *pink and yellow and blue*; key passages had been highlighted with fluorescent markers, *also pink and yellow and blue. Was there a secret code at work in the trio of colors?* one weekly asked.

The three sisters were seeking to have the book banned, arguing that *it was the doctor who planted the idea of a pleasant, effortless death in the mother of four's head, and misled the vulnerable young woman regarding the efficacy of Nembutal.*

Although *the dog-eared copy had been confiscated as probable evidence*, one paper got hold of some journal entries that Erin had supposedly written in the book. The journals were clearly fabricated, turning her death into a sentimental daytime soap opera, except for a line or two, which I wanted to believe she actually wrote, that made Erin come off like some bleak philosopher: *"We're all involuntarily admitted into the*

*world," the doomed mother pronounced in her last entry, scribbled hurriedly
before she rushed to the airport. "Suicide allows us to be discharged from the
world, voluntarily."*

I read up a little on that doctor myself, ordering some of his books from
my local library. He's somewhat of an inventor. He's designed these
suicide machines—the technical term is *euthanasia device*—to assist
people in the process of ending their lives.

There's one called the Deliverance Machine, which, from what I
could gather, is a software program that asks the participant a number
of questions and, if you give the right answers, automatically injects you
with a shot of barbiturates. It's intended for individuals suffering from
incurable, painful diseases, but the Deliverance Machine would have an
allure for individuals subject to suffering in all its shapes and forms; such
a machine could be of use to the individual who, for whatever reason,
has suicidal ideation, for whom suicide is the idée fixe . . .

There was a picture of this strange machine: an old-fashioned gray
laptop hooked up to a device in a carrier case that resembled a portable
record player—perhaps it was the headphones. As I gazed at the contrap-
tion, an erasing device if ever there was one, I wondered about the voice
that asks the questions. I imagined it was vocoded, soothing. Or like the
smooth, unmodulated voice of an airline hostess who does those safety
videos. What if you gave the answers the machine wanted to hear and
were taken to the final screen, but then changed your mind at the last
minute—was there a back arrow?

These appliances are pricey and hard to come by, so Nitschke has
written other books, DIY guides for the handyman who wants to fix
everything. These books come with diagrams and simple instructions,
showcasing assisted suicide gadgets anyone can make, potentially, *out of
everyday household products lying around unused* such as gas bottles from
barbecues, nitrogen canisters *that can also be utilized to brew your own
beer*, plastic shopping bags with draw cords (the correct term is *Exit
Bags*), rubber tubing, strong tape. Put it all together, and hey, presto!

I have to say I became quite engrossed in these inventions. I could feel Erin reading along with me, over my shoulder, tracking each line with her finger. Looking at the pictures gave me a cold, shiny feeling, one I had not felt in a long time. I had to force myself to stop. I'd planned on renewing the books, but another member of the library had requested them. Not wanting to risk a fine, I returned the books to the Venice library before their due date. I made photocopies of the instructions for a couple of the simplest machines. I'm not very good with my hands, so, luckily, I don't think I would be capable of building one myself.

Maybe Erin felt the same. That's why, instead of taking her life in the privacy of her own home, or in a little cottage down south, she took the cab to Perth International Airport and hopped on a plane.

How much luggage did she bring? I assume she traveled light. The duration of the flight from Perth to Tokyo is approximately ten hours and eighteen minutes. Tokyo to San Francisco takes approximately nine hours and twenty minutes. San Francisco to Mexico City is approximately four hours and twenty-five minutes, and from there the flight to Tijuana is another three hours and twenty-one minutes—*the exact time of each flight depends on the speed of the winds.* That's a long haul, not to mention stopovers. Erin would not have reached her destination until a day or so later, or earlier, or whatever, what with all the changes in time zones.

What time zone is the afterlife in? Erin allegedly wrote that as well, in the index of Nitschke's book, next to *Nembutal* and *nitrogen canister.*

More importantly, how did Erin dress for the journey? In my one dream of her, she decided to take, as the saying goes, *nothing but the clothes on her back.* She did not have a clothes iron so she came over to our house and I helped her set up the ironing board in the laundry and she ironed her Santa Maria tunic. I told her the school uniform was *a good choice, loose-fitting. Make sure you unplug the iron,* she told me. She put on the green tunic and left for the airport. Whatever Erin chose to wear, I hope she dressed comfortably.

Erin flew to her death, like Mike, but with greater intention. *I want to be as untraceable as nitrogen:* more of Erin's "thoughts," before the paper's "exclusive" was exposed as a fake.

The reasoning behind her choice is beyond me, beyond everyone, far beyond the sorrow of her mother and sisters, her husband and children, a secret code known only to Erin, yet I can't help but . . . admire her method. I don't mean the Nembutal, I mean the trip. In classical fiction, the journey to the underworld is grueling, perilous, and Erin . . . mimicked that undertaking, mirrored death's steps, doubled them.

To go far away to end your own life. I could say more on the subject of suicide in general, but it will take me off course, divert me from my own intentions. So can we save that conversation for a rainy day?

There is something, though, that I need to get off my chest.

Details have been coming back to me while I've been telling you Erin's story, in what I consider chronological order, and I may have mixed up one or two things. For one, Erin was not the only blonde; I'm pretty sure Caitlin was blonde too. I'm beginning to think she was the youngest, not Erin; Caitlin came over with her mother as well, possibly more often than her older sister. And that incident involving the Q-tip might have happened in reverse: Erin may have punctured Caitlin's eardrum. I honestly don't recall.

I suppose I could ask my mom next time I talk to her on the phone. She mentions Mrs. O'Kane now and then, says she hasn't been herself since Erin's death; she lives in a small house with her stray dogs, goes to bed by six o'clock.

As for the afternoon with the *Playboy*, neither sister was present; that took place with a boy from my neighborhood, Mark, who, like Erin, had dirty-blonde hair and a snub nose and was perpetually sunburned.

I'm no better than those journalists, I guess; I've offered a misleading impression. No, I've imparted a false account of Erin, warped and twisted her truth out of shape, like death distorts us beyond recognition.

All I have left are more questions:

On the customs form, what address did Erin give as her final destination? A customs officer surely inquired about *the purpose of her trip.* How did she respond? What did she declare?

And how did she spend all those hours in the air? Twenty-seven hours, twenty-four minutes, if my arithmetic is right. Did she sleep most of the time? Aware of the void that was awaiting her, did she stay up every minute, taking full advantage of the meals and the beverages and the snacks, of the in-flight entertainment? Or did she just stare at the video monitor that tracks the plane's movement, indicating how many miles and hours to go until you get to your location?

Erin is, more than ever, irretrievable. If she could hear what I was saying, I doubt she would even want to be retrieved. There is no black box for the dead's thoughts. Her thoughts on that journey are lost to us.

But now that I've acknowledged the instability of my memory, let's embellish, let's distort freely, in this story of the only blonde in a family of redheads, of my one true childhood friend: before she got to Tijuana (and she didn't stop there . . .), Erin experienced an intoxicating sensation, hard to put into words—no, make that impossible—something along the lines of . . . *liberty.* She could not remember the last time she felt so light, and, wishing she could go on flying forever, wrote on the back of the customs form *maybe this is what death is like, always moving, always between places, enclosed in a pressurized state of weightless, dreamlike suspension.*

Regulations

Sometimes I feel like a ghost, drifting through life in a weightless fashion. Do you ever feel that? I don't just mean a ghost in the sense of an apparition who appears to living persons in a gauzy form and makes them go agh! which would be more tangible, but a ghost in the sense of a false image, a secondary image, often faint. I sort of . . . float along the washed-out pastel boulevards of Culver City, among other actual human beings. I feel like I could float . . . right through you.

On the back of my map of Holy Cross there is a list of instructions, informing patrons what they can and cannot do. No dogs. No artificial flowers. Only a certain type of vase permitted. *The construction of trenches around graves is strictly prohibited.* No idling or loafing or *any other form of boisterous activity.*

There are security guards enforcing these rules during visiting hours, 8:00 a.m. to 5:00 p.m., Monday through Sunday. I've seen them chase off the skater boys who come to the cemetery, dressed in their black hoodies and their skeleton-patterned clothes like brand-name memento mori, to skate down the hill: the spinning, humming sound of a skateboard approaching; that could be a death omen. I wish the guards would spend more time regulating the traffic; I don't know the speed limit for a cemetery, and those drivers might be grieving, but most cars clearly exceed the limit. One time a guard even came up to me and asked what I was doing. He seemed to think I was loitering. He eyed my black bag, as though I were hiding a knife in it. I told him I was from the university, doing research, which was sort of true.

Holy Cross claims the directives help *maintain the beauty and dignity of the cemetery*. I think they're being disingenuous, and the rules are to maintain order, form, structure, in the face of death's chaos, formlessness, disarray: *Death*, the great disintegrator, the gnarly unmaker. I just don't see much beauty there, or here, do you? All I've seen is a bureaucratic method designed to counter *Death*'s awesome humiliation.

Luckily, the guards never bothered me again. In my black shirt and trousers, they probably assume I'm in mourning or just some harmless white-collar worker with a buried Goth past. I'm not sure if either supposition is true, but I adhere to these principles of conduct, which apply only to visitors, not the cemetery's residents, who must find the whirr and skitter of those skateboard wheels annoying, like the constant movement of upstairs neighbors. We are obliged to display reverence for the dead, but they must feel no such need. We must comply with these regulations, but within the confines of the cemetery, the dead have been given free reign.

The University of Disintegration

I have this recurring thought that I don't want to even think,
let alone say out loud, but here goes: for most people, the
problem of death is one of excess. For me, it is an issue of
scarcity. My predicament is a little different; actually, it's
reversed: it's not that there has been too much death in my
life. The problem is there hasn't been nearly enough.

Every so often I wonder if I'm looking in the right direction. A cemetery might not be the best place to comprehend death. After all, the dead aren't exactly effusive when it comes to conversation. They keep their cards close to their bony chests. It's possible I'm looking too far. I could just stay within the confines of the university, which reflects the cemetery in its glass surface.

I won't bore you with the details of my work there, but as soon as you open the tinted glass-plate doors, ignoring the sign in the lower-right corner that states *this building is cleaned with cleaning agents that may contain chemicals known by the state of California to cause cancer, birth defects and other forms of reproductive harm,* you sense there's more than enough death to go around.

Within the building's overly air-conditioned environment, which gives you a sneak preview of algor mortis, that postmortem escapade in which there is a steady decline in a corpse's body temperature until it matches the ambient temperature that surrounds it, the students, they tell me things. Most of the time I'm like you; I'm so quiet people feel the urge to . . . confide in me.

Take Rose. Back in Georgia, her best friend Kate was kidnapped at gunpoint by two meth-heads. The men made her drive to an ATM, then on to another, and another, forcing her to make withdrawals, promising to let her go, then reneging on their promise. Here in LA, Rose's other best friend Maria leapt from the observation deck in the tower of City Hall, whose thirty-two stories made it the tallest building in the city until 1964 and whose art deco architecture is widely admired.

Stacey was declared clinically dead not once, but twice: OD'd from too much coke and crystal and speed. I'm surprised she survived; she's such a slight thing. She told me she didn't see anything while she was dead, and that *coming back to life was nothing to write home about*; she didn't like receiving mouth to mouth from a stranger.

After Ryan had a stroke, he lay unconscious on the floor of his apartment for two days until a neighbor found him. He was in a coma for a month. He's doing better now, though he says he feels like he's moving underwater and his speech is noticeably slurred. His range of vocabulary is returning, but he still misidentifies words. For example, he calls an *incinerator* a *disintegrator*.

And what about Carlos? He went whitewater rafting with his father down some river in Northern California. He was *stoked, it was such a rush*, but the boat turned over. Carlos watched as his dad went under, got stuck beneath some rocks, and was washed away in gushing foam.

There are plenty more stories where these come from. It's as if being on intimate terms with death is an unwritten prerequisite to be accepted to the university.

Don't get me wrong. The students are spacey, hyperdistracted. We blame this on technology, and in class they hide behind their laptops, like glowing headstones of the upright variety, but I suggest that it's hard to concentrate on what's going on in front of you when there's another zone to think about, where your friends have gone, where we might be heading, where something is or isn't happening.

And despite their abstractedness, these students, they're so real and pure. You can hear death in their voices, see it in their faces; you know, I can see death in your face. They're all so frail, emotionally, like you could touch any one of them gently on the shoulder and she or he would crumble into fine powder. I don't envy my students—but actually, I do.

Somehow they're less . . . self-conscious than me, more open, more sincere in their hopes and their dreams. Carlos, Rose, Stacey, Ryan: they speak straight from the heart. When I try to do that my words get snagged on the walls of my arteries, washed away in my bloodstream; the sentiments are lost long before they leave my mouth. After forty years, I'm still under the impression that I'm not quite real and, as a consequence, I'm not going to die. The student body's . . . proximity to death makes them more connected to life than I'll ever be.

Chris, a Recipe

When it comes to the dead, there are different kinds of stories: a biography tends to be exhaustive; an obituary is more selective; a eulogy heaps praise upon the dead, until they are buried in our praise; an epitaph is a miniature biography, like a skull shrunk by a headhunter. What you should notice is the gradual magnification of events, the whittling away of details, the increasing application of pressure. Each story can be told in descending order, until there is no such thing as stories.

So I don't get out much anymore. My life has been reduced to work, home, cemetery.

I used to hang out at this bar in Venice, the Rooster-Fish, which is just down the street from our house. The last time I went was about a year ago. I met up with my friends Richard and Arturo. They live in the neighborhood. Richard's moody and Arturo's melancholy so I get on fairly well with them. They keep to themselves—but they've been very good to me, especially when Tim's away and I go a little stir-crazy. They cook for me and get me out of the house, take me to places in LA that I've never been. Like the observation deck at the top of City Hall. I haven't seen them in a while—I suppose I should look them up.

Anyway, we were at the bar last summer on a Sunday afternoon. Architecturally speaking, the Rooster-Fish is a bright aqua box. Inside it's dark and dingy, and no matter what time of day, it stinks of detergent and stale beer. There's a small back patio where it doesn't smell as bad.

We sat outside at a wooden table and I had a vodka and tonic or two and we all smoked some weed.

That's another way in which Richard is generous: he's never without weed and he doles it out freely. He's not one to talk about his inner state but he told me once that he believed marijuana was essential to cope with *the rigors of life*. He revealed that he tried to give up, but he comes from a family of people *who take life too seriously; life has taken its toll on them* and he could see this happening to him and he didn't want it to happen, so he resumed his habit, or as he refers to it, *his solution*.

I was feeling ready to take on life's rigors myself that day. On Sundays at the Fish, they have a barbeque, and I ate three hotdogs, which are my favorite food in the world. When I eat them I feel like I'm at a funfair, like Coney Island. I was a little high and I started going on about how good they were, saying that if I was going to be executed and the prison guards offered me a last meal, I would choose hotdogs. The hotdogs might help me forget the fact that I was about to die.

This got me thinking about the form of execution I would choose, if the prison warden gave me the choice, providing me with a certain freedom over the ordinary humans who live with the misconception that they are free, yet wait around for whatever horrible form of death nature dishes out. Surely I would go for the quickest and the least painful method, like lethal injection, something nice and humane. Definitely not firing squad or beheading or hanging or the electric chair. Or would firing squad be okay? At least I would be blindfolded. And in the old Foreign Legion movies, they always give the condemned guy a cigarette, which I would probably accept, even though I don't smoke cigarettes. Then, before they fire, the head officer asks if you have any last words.

I didn't share this daydream with my friends. I explored it . . . inwardly. I began to wonder what my last words would be, but from within my pot haze I couldn't come up with any.

Richard and Arturo are what you would call *regulars*: a host of other people kept sitting down and joining us, coming and going. Everyone was chatting about this or that.

Conversation with strangers at a bar is demanding; you have to figure out what to say to a person you've just met. You need to identify topics of general interest or talk extemporaneously about nothing in particular. The exchange is informal yet structured: you're meant to listen and then respond, listen and respond. You want to keep it light. You should hold the other person's focus and also be attentive to what they're saying. There's a lot to consider.

Basically, I'm not very good at it. More often than not, the individual I find myself forced to converse with gets a funny look on their face and says *nice to meet you* and that they'll *be back in a moment* and then they get up and flee. Communicating outside a bar is worse; you must have guessed by now I don't excel at human relations. Sure, I can talk to you, but what we have . . . it's unusual. You're technically a stranger, but I feel more comfortable around you than I do around myself. And though I only have one interest, and it's quite specific, it's an interest we have in common.

So while Richard and Arturo were being convivial, I went a little quiet. The weed aided and abetted this state; it seems to cut off the part of my brain that is responsible for language, which is undoubtedly the drug's main appeal.

Sitting there in the shade, I wouldn't say I was at one with the world, but separate from it, severed, silent, and content as the dead.

I assume I was introduced to a number of people that afternoon; however, the only person whose likeness I've retained is this guy Chris. I wouldn't recall him at all, except for the fact that . . . But I'm getting ahead of myself. I'm about to spoil the surprise, ruin the story, though it should be apparent that all my stories are already ruined.

As Chris approached the table, I noticed that he was physically un-remarkable. Short and stocky, with gingerish hair, the ends stiff with dried clumps of gel. Though he did have a friendly face. Some people's faces are closed to you, sealed shut, like the wood panels you see nailed to the window frames of abandoned houses; I know my face is, but Chris had an open, welcoming face.

When he sat down, Richard did the necessary introductions and mentioned that Chris was a fellow Canadian—they both came from one of those icy uninhabited provinces—and a very good chef who worked in one of the restaurants on Abbot Kinney. I don't remember how he characterized me.

While Chris and Arturo were catching up, Richard leaned in and changed his tune. He warned me not to broach the topic of cooking or food: if you did, Chris would go on endlessly; he would give you an extensive rundown of his favorite recipes, explaining every measurement, every ingredient, and every step: you couldn't get him to stop.

"It's deeply, deeply tedious," Richard said, rubbing the tiny ivory skull on the top of his cane, a tool he uses for his bad hip as well as for its dandyish effect. "Whatever you do, don't get him started."

Richard and I both prefer books to reality, and I told him that it sounded like one of those long-winded scenes in a nineteenth-century novel, where Levin pontificates on the latest farming techniques and agrarian innovations in *Anna Karenina*, or in *Middlemarch* when Tertius Lydgate or Dorothea's bumbling uncle Mr. Arthur Brooke speculate on modern medical discoveries and reformist economic policies and the intricacies of county politics, and even those early twentieth-century novels that reek of the nineteenth century, like in *The Magic Mountain*, when that Italian is lecturing Hans Castorp on the political and philo-sophical nature of *the cloud over Europe*, except it's Chris expounding on the nuances and contradictions of the latest culinary trends.

Or did I keep these ideas to myself?

Either way, I did what Richard explicitly told me not to do.

I leaned over and asked Chris if he could recommend a recipe, as I was hoping to extend my repertoire.

Just as Richard predicted, Chris began to describe in great detail a dish he had cooked that morning: a recipe of his grandma's. The dish was quite simple but his instructions were painstaking; he delineated each measurement, each ingredient, each step.

As Chris held forth, I pretended to listen, an act at which I'm quite convincing, while barely taking a word in.

For once I was genuinely curious. I just couldn't . . . concentrate. All I can tell you about the actual recipe is that it involved potatoes and an oven. It felt like Chris took the same amount of time to explain the recipe as it would take him to make the dish itself, from beginning to end, including preparation and cooking time, but that may have been the marijuana, which is known to affect space-time perception.

I tuned out for a while, then tuned back in when I heard Chris mention Felix, Richard and Arturo's parrot. Felix is a medium-sized bird, colorful and vicious. (He bit me on the finger once. On a separate occasion he bit Richard on the nipple and he bled.)

Chris asked how old Felix was; I don't recall the bird's exact age, but Richard said that most parrots live for forty to sixty-plus years.

"That's why we got a parrot, that was the attraction," he said, "because of the life span. But," he added, "we both worry about Felix—who'll look after him if something happens to us?"

"I will" said Chris, taking a drag from Richard's marble pipe. "I love that bird."

A parrot can easily outlive you, I thought, it can be in mourning for you despite its gaudy feathers. A parrot could be your coffin bearer, and could squawk out some touching words at your memorial.

"Wow," I said—an expression I used constantly as a kid, and still use, when the occasion calls. It's such a convenient term when faced with the world.

I was alert to the fact of the bird's longevity, but Chris was in awe.

"Wow," he kept saying, as if he were a parrot and I had just taught him this word. "Wow."

We kept smoking. The angle of the sun kept shifting and so did I. Chris excused himself; did I say good-bye? External time seemed to lengthen though Sunday came and went.

It's interesting how in this life you meet so many people only once. The encounter is brief and you immediately forget them. I feel like most individuals fall into this category.

But there is a second category, composed of those individuals you encounter and forget, and then, something terrible befalls them, and you hear about it and suddenly you remember and say, *oh yes, I met him.*

About six months ago, I ran into Richard at the local farmers market, which is held in the library parking lot every Friday morning. I don't go there much anymore, either; it closes at eleven and it's hard to get out of the house at that hour.

Richard was wheeling his bike through the market and we walked together for a few minutes. When I asked him how he had been, his face kind of crumpled. He told me that he was at the bar the night before and had heard that a friend of his, Chris, had died.

As soon as Richard said the name, I knew whom he meant. I hardly ever remember the name of someone the first time, especially a human as average as Chris. I guess under certain conditions humans are compelled to remember.

"Is that the chef?" I asked.

"Yeah," Richard said, "how did you know?"

I reminded him that he had introduced me to Chris.

"I'm sorry to hear about that," I said as we navigated our way through the crowd and their bundles of organic produce. This was an appropriate response, one we feel obligated to say. Then I posed *that* question, the one we cannot help but ask, "So how did he die?"

Richard's face got all creased again. He informed me that Chris had died in a car accident. Although Chris was in his midforties, he had just obtained his first driver's license. He finally decided to learn how to drive, after years of resisting. He only had the license a few days, when he entered the off-ramp of a freeway (or did Richard say he exited the on-ramp? Is that even possible?). In any case, he made a fatal error, screwed up some of the ground rules of road safety. Chris's death was the mistake of an inexperienced driver and could have easily been avoided.

"I had seen him at the bar only a couple nights ago," Richard said. "He took me outside and showed me his car, this beautiful pale-blue Cadillac. I heard the car was totaled."

"Wow," I said. I don't believe that's an appropriate idiom to use in this circumstance, but it's a convenient term when faced with death.

Richard's face was still creased. I looked off . . . in the distance? Into empty space? I don't like being near other humans when their bodies are blurting out their emotions. Corpses are easier to be around; they're so calm. I glanced down at his hands and noticed they were trembling; he clutched the handlebars of his bicycle to still them.

It was clear that Richard was shaken up by the incident. Even his hands gave him away. And me? Objectively, I could see this was a tragedy, but I had only met Chris once. My memory of him was . . . scarcely a memory. My feelings were muted, so soft and low it's possible I didn't feel anything. Though aren't we always feeling something?

What's weird is that I had been reconsidering going for my license. I took the test years ago but failed when I ran a red and nearly hit an old lady.

"You can't go into a fugue state," the instructor yelled.

It's not like I was doing it on purpose. I just kept . . . ignoring the roads and the lights and the signs and sort of . . . sinking into my imagination.

I had even been studying for the learners, but I interpreted Chris's death as an omen, good and bad, that I should stick to walking and public transportation.

Richard said he had to get back home—he teaches philosophy and he's been working on a book forever. He finds the process of writing excruciating. He's told me what the book is about countless times, but its theme continues to escape me. We stopped near a stall that sells potatoes, in every color you can imagine. I thought about them growing underground, in the dark, in the dirt, their corpsy consistency and then I thought of the recipe Chris shared with me at the bar. I began to explain its implications but Richard shot me a look, like what a strange thing to remember, and said he really had to go. There are some insights you just can't divulge, maybe most that are of consequence. But let me tell you.

It was like Chris was trying to pass on the recipe. You know how families have those secret recipes with a special ingredient that are handed down from one generation to the next? I have a hunch that's what Chris was trying to do; he wanted to teach me the recipe so it could live on, through me.

Which implies that on a certain level . . . *he knew*. He sensed that the situation of his birth, the result of a collision between two forces, bloody, accidental, would lead directly to the situation of his death, the result of a collision between two forces, bloody, accidental. He bought that beautiful pale-blue Cadillac to die in, to go out in style in.

That's why he went on and on when it came to the subject of food: Chris intuited he wasn't going to be around for long; he had to get the most out of his mouth's ability to speak, while there was still time.

And though on a conscious level he must have been insensible to this knowledge sleeping inside him, I swear Chris had this fervent look in his eyes, counter to his measured delivery: his eyes let slip that he was desperate to transfer that recipe.

Chris chose me as the bearer of his wisdom, however modest. Of course this is just a hypothesis. I could maintain that his recipe was too secret to be conveyed, too esoteric, but essentially, he picked the wrong guy. Unless I picked him, because I knew, somehow I was . . . aware that I had to take advantage of this opportunity to speak with a man whom I erroneously took to be undistinguished. Or perhaps I just asked about cooking because I was totally high and I do enjoy my food.

Listen to me, now I'm the one going on, as if it's me who wants to take advantage of speech, or there's something urgent I wish to convey to you, *while I still have the time*, which accounts for the growing fervency of my voice.

Let's cut through all the metaphysics and skip the story altogether. I can tell you exactly how Chris could have avoided his death. He should have been paying attention while he drove. Just like I should have been paying attention while he spoke to me. It's too late for both of us.

If I keep to the facts, I end up with a narrative that's a cross between an obituary and a limerick, concise enough to fit on a headstone: *Chris was a chef. He explained recipes at interminable length. At the age of 44, he took his driver's test; he passed. A week later he died in a car accident. All his recipes died with him.*

My Coffin

I used to have so many obsessions, I couldn't keep up with them. But then I came to see they were all secondary obsessions, distracting me from my primary obsession, D____h, which makes the function of obsession inevitable, indispensable. Without death there would be no need to obsess. This could mean I've matured, or something else entirely.

There's a retail space at the corner of Lincoln and Washington Boulevards in Venice that has been, in this order: a pet store, a coffin store, a skate shop.

I've visited the business in all its manifestations.

I have encountered, in this order, the odors of dogs, wood polish, boys.

The word *coffin* has several denotations.

It can refer to the part of a horse's foot that features the so-called *coffin bone*. We don't have this bone in our feet.

In the early days of printing, *the coffin* was the wooden frame around the bed of the press.

The word comes from the Old French *cofin*, meaning *little basket*.

Coffin can be used as a verb, as in *his lithe body was coffined*, but this is getting too circular.

I will disregard *a coffin's* connotations.

For our purposes, *a coffin* is a long, narrow box, typically constructed out of wood, in which a dead body is placed.

When the space on Lincoln was California Caskets, I would gaze in the window whenever I walked by, but I only went inside there once.

As I pushed the door open, and a little bell rang, I could still smell dry pet food, an olfactory remnant from the store's days as California Pet Supplies. A man came out from a back office, dressed in a dark, cheap suit.

Do you need any help? he asked in a phony solemn voice and I told him *I was just browsing*—as soon as I said this I realized how odd it must have sounded, but it was too late to take it back. And I couldn't tell him why I was really there: I wanted to find a coffin with my name written all over it.

I didn't stay long. The children's coffins, decorated with waterfalls and castles and unicorns, as if the afterlife is some fantasy kingdom, were disconcerting. The manager was watching me the whole time, as if I might steal something, tuck a coffin down the front of my trousers or into my pocket.

The question of choice and selection was puzzling. What's more important, the coffin's interior or exterior? The models that came in bronze and steel, with their polish and chrome and their suggestion of speed, made me feel like I was in a car showroom. A coffin is a mode of transportation.

I know this about coffins: a half-couch casket opens at the top, so you can only see the face of the corpse and the shirt he is wearing, while a full-couch opens completely, so you can also see the corpse's trousers and the shoes on his feet. As soon as the lid is closed, the corpse must breathe a sigh of relief.

Some years ago, I was walking along the Venice Boardwalk when I came across a guy selling coffins. I kid you not. His stall was squeezed in between a stall selling Rastafarian paraphernalia and one specializing in skull-shaped bongs. He was sitting on a striped folding chair next to a sign that said *Ataudes Baratos/Cheap Coffins: Pagos Fáciles/Easy Payments*. Right behind him in the parking lot was a car. The rear door was open and two coffins were sticking out.

I wandered over to inspect his merchandise. The coffins were made from a reddish wood. They looked slightly scratched. On a small table there was a laminated menu, like the menus you get in a Chinese restaurant, but with pictures of coffins.

I went back several times—I used to go to the boardwalk regularly, before Holy Cross became my stomping ground—but I never saw him again. I don't think he had the proper license required of boardwalk vendors. I liked the concept, selecting your coffin after a day in the sun. Yet I sensed there was something fishy about his business, despite the fact or perhaps because he told me that all his coffins were *in excellent condition*.

The death industry is more exacting than I am in its use of terminology: a coffin has six or eight sides and follows the lines of the human body; a casket has four sides, and does not.

There is a standard size for coffins, but if you're concerned that it might be a tight fit, an undertaker will be happy to measure your corpse from one side of the bend in the elbow to the other side, while your hands are resting on your abdomen. There's something indecorous about measuring a corpse for their coffin, like measuring the inseam of a man's leg at a gentleman's tailor.

A coffin is also a retail space; a dead body is a commodity. Online, there are coffins with full-length mirrors attached to the inside of the lid, so the dead can check their appearance from time to time, monitor their transformation from your average corpse to full-blown skeleton to something beyond bones.

So I had this dream where I bought myself a coffin, from a mail order catalog. It was a catalog for men's underwear, but at the back there was a coffin section. At night, I would look at the sexy photos of men in their white jockey shorts and then at the coffins, which were even sexier. Coffins are unseemly. Being caught in your coffin is like someone catching you in your underpants.

I don't remember the name of the model I chose, but I do recall the caption beneath the photo: *A sound investment for your future.*

I ordered the coffin, which took ages to arrive, and when it finally did, it looked nothing like the picture; the product was deeply disappointing, as all goods bought from catalogs are destined to be. In fact, I wasn't even sure it was a coffin. It looked more like a complex, menacing, multitiered spice rack.

I grabbed the catalog, which I had stashed in a hole cut into my mattress. I called up and demanded my money back, but as the customer service representative informed me: *All coffins are nonrefundable and nonreturnable.*

The Caretaker's Wife

*"I don't know why you're so fascinated with death," she said.
"You'll find out all about it soon enough."*

On the other side of the hill, beyond the mausoleum, there's a blue stucco house where the caretaker lives. That's something I would like to show you.

When I was a kid I used to have this fantasy that my family lived in a cemetery and my dad was the caretaker. I don't know where this scenario came from—I probably read it in a book. It struck me as very romantic: to have an entire cemetery as your backyard, to play hide-and-seek with your friends among the tombstones; to take your best friend by the hand and lead him behind a tombstone, so that no one else can see. When my father died I would take over and become the caretaker myself; I would soon learn that looking after a cemetery is a great responsibility.

I've never caught sight of Holy Cross's custodian, who, I imagine, does not have a spare moment in his day, but I've seen a woman who must be his wife. One afternoon I was walking by the house when a lady came out the front door. She was quite shrunken. Old people shrink, right? I think it has something to do with gravity pushing at the spaces between the bones of the spine, so everything gets compacted and jammed together. Or the bones just can't be bothered to grow anymore; with death approaching, they don't see the point. The woman was wearing a housecoat that looked like it was going to drown her. She was carrying something in her hand, which was misshapen, slightly claw-like.

122

Somewhat unsteady on her feet, she went over to the red and yellow roses that mark the perimeter of their yard, the boundaries of their property. She began pruning with the tool in her hand, a pair of clippers. Unaware of my presence, absorbed in her work, I stood there and watched her. As she pruned, cutting away the dead and unnecessary parts of the rosebush, she hummed a tune to herself. She seemed very pleased, perhaps because her roses were so healthy, big as baby's skulls—you know what they say about bones being good fertilizer. Though her happiness may have been derived from a more general source, sheer gratitude at waking up each day in a cemetery; how rewarding it must be working alongside the dead, how peaceful it must be sleeping beside the dead, who fertilize your dreams so extravagantly, as they are profligate by nature, and unconcerned with waste.

I'm trying to be a little friendlier with my fellow human beings, and I told her how lovely her roses were. At first she didn't seem to hear, so I said it again and she looked up at me and didn't look pleased at all. She just glowered at me, like the dead must glare at the living when we enter a graveyard and encroach on their territory. I didn't take offense; I expect you become withdrawn when you're around the dead all day every day; the dead's taciturn nature feels normal while the living and their drive toward communication seems pathological, creepy. The caretaker's wife didn't say anything and returned to her task, removing the superfluous elements of the rosebush, with the goal of future abundance, a task that once again absorbed her.

Cooper's Story

Birth certificates and death certificates are also stories: empirical, clinical. The forms are quite similar. Both documents ask for identifying data: names and dates and times and locations. Both are interested in causality and required by law. Neither document bears our signature. It's as if we refuse to verify the authenticity of our birth or our death. These documents are said to be essential yet have very little to do with us. The law will accept the signatures of those remote individuals we call parents and the signatures of strangers.

Cooper turned blue. He was the first child of my sister Jeannine and her husband, Paul. He was born on December 16, 1996, and he died on December 23, 1996. Born on a Monday, died the following Monday. He lived for a week, so there's very little to tell. How much can happen to someone who's only around for seven days? I've been keeping you longer than I intended but this one should be short, I promise.

My mother called here twice in a week. That's unusual. The first call announced the birth of Cooper; the second, his death. Actually, I think there was a third call, a voicemail left in between the two, where Mom said something was wrong.

For the first couple of days, everything was fine—a boy, a son, a grandchild—but while my sister was in the hospital, she noticed Cooper was a funny color. She asked the nurse about it and the doctors did some tests and then they gave her the prognosis.

124

Cooper had blue baby syndrome. This syndrome is caused by a heart defect known as Tetralogy of Fallot. It sounds like the name of some medieval knight. The blood doesn't flow properly, doesn't receive enough oxygen, which gives blood its redness apparently, hence the blue tinge to the baby's extremities: lips, fingers, toes. In many instances the condition is treatable, but in this case, due to the complicated structure of Cooper's heart, and the size of the hole in the two bottom chambers, there was nothing they could do.

After that, things moved quickly. Jeannine and Paul were allowed to take Cooper home. I don't know how they spent those remaining days, except on the Sunday. According to my mother, they invited everyone over to their house in Hilton to have a barbeque and spend some time with Cooper. The day was a scorcher. Everyone came then everyone left and Cooper died, in the early hours of Monday morning.

The funeral took place just before Christmas. If he died on the twenty-third, it must have been held on Christmas Eve. Can funerals happen at such short notice? Don't they require planning and advance warning? I wonder if I have the correct dates for Cooper's birth and his death. Are dates important? Cooper was alive for exactly one week, of this I am certain.

I probably should have thought about flying home, to be there for my sister, but I didn't even consider it. Remember, I was over nine thousand miles away. I was caught up in my new life.

Mom said the coffin was so small, she couldn't bear to look at it. Even though it was light, they had four coffin bearers, one on each corner. Because of the coffin's compact dimensions, the men had to walk close together and kept on bumping into one another.

Which means my mother must have called a fourth time, to tell me about the funeral. Or she mentioned it when I rang to wish her and Dad and my brother Andrew a Merry Christmas.

I only have the vaguest memory of these calls, which might explain my poor grasp of key details, but I do remember that during one, I was taken back to the morning Mom came into the kitchen to tell me about Gran. The same abstract mystery was being presented to me. Except now we weren't in the same room and I was a grown man and we were talking about an infant, not an old lady, and it was me who was on the opposite side of the world.

I also recall how the tenor of my mother's voice changed over the course of that week. At first it was breathy and excited; during the second call, it was hesitant and full of pauses; by the fourth call, her voice had fractured until it broke off in two.

Some photos of Cooper came in the mail (which raises the question: Did I learn some of this narrative by way of my mother's letters, her spidery handwriting, rather than through the tremors of her voice?).

A few were taken at the hospital, before anyone was aware of his heart condition. In those pictures Cooper is pink and wrinkled and looks perplexed, like all babies do. Whoever's holding him—Jeannine, my mother, Paul, my father—looks euphoric, overjoyed.

But then there are the photos taken later, that Sunday at my sister's house, in the shade of a jacaranda tree in the backyard. Although the location provides a clue, you can tell by the . . . shredded expressions on people's faces that the situation has shifted. Everyone knows what's going to happen.

Surely one of the most joyous aspects of the arrival of a newborn is the uncertainty of their fate. But when their fate has been decided, from the get-go, surely this is unbearable.

As members of my family hold Cooper and pose for whoever took these snapshots, they're smiling, but their eyes are red. Some are weeping. Others are attempting to hide their grief but are unable to.

Cooper is no longer pink; his skin is as blue as the pale-blue crocheted blanket he's wrapped in, and slightly purplish, like the stray jacaranda flowers that have fallen on his head.

And his expression has changed. While the adults are tearing up, their features torn apart by what they're . . . feeling, he is, at least on the surface—the surface of the photograph and the surface of his skin—impassive, stoic. Everything about him is unreadable, yet he appears to have acquired a certain . . . erudition.

We want existence to drag on and on, so that it trails behind us, like those demons who are said to prey on pregnant women and whose entrails drag behind them, but perhaps seven days is enough. Perhaps, in that swift transition from womb to world to coffin, from the pink void to the bright void to the void that we presume will be black, you can experience every aspect of existence, you can learn an awful lot, possibly all there is to know.

I still have those photos. They're in this beat-up little metal lunchbox, where I keep other pictures and postcards and letters. I haven't looked at them in years. I don't think I care to.

Cooper's death was like one of those fairy tales I devoured as a kid, in which no one is safe from evil or harm: *There was a newborn child, and a witch came along and placed a curse on him, and over the course of a week, the child turned the loveliest shade of blue, and by the end of the week, he was old . . .*

Or a story from the Old Testament: *She prayed to God that her firstborn be a son and be beautiful, and in his goodness God gave her a beautiful son, and then he decided to test her . . .*

I suspect you have to be pretty strong to deal with something like this. To get through it. My sister was. I can't imagine what it was like, carrying this being inside you for nine months, and then he finally arrives and you're elated, you have his tender body in your arms, and then in just over a week you're burying your firstborn in a hole in the ground, while he's still warm; you can feel the trace of him turning and flipping inside of you. You still recall the preternatural sensation of him . . . occupying you. And now you're a void. How do you pull yourself out of such sadness?

How do you keep from going mad over such a thing?

Jeannine and I talked about Cooper, around six months after his death, when I was back home for a visit. The trip was meant to last for only three weeks, and although I was not enjoying myself, I kept changing my return date; for a while I was not clear if I was going to come back to Los Angeles at all, but for some reason I did.

I had been staying with my parents, but that night I stayed at Jeannine and Paul's house. As we sat on the porch, Jeannine brought up Cooper's last night. I like to think that I introduced the topic, asked her how she was doing. She said the day never cooled down, and that she and Paul sat outside so Cooper could hear the evening sounds, the cicadas and birds, see the stars, cram in a little more experience.

She said they were ready to have another baby. My sister was filled with trepidation but she told me she had a dream, not long after Cooper died, where she was in a plane crash. The plane crashed into the sea, near the shore, and everyone drowned except for her: she emerged from the aircraft wearing one of my mom's cotton nighties, blue as Cooper's skin, and waded back to shore, safe and sound. When she woke up somehow she knew it would be okay.

She and Paul have three boys now: Remy, Marley, Fyfe. From the photos she sends me, they appear to have Paul's long limbs and Jeannine's soft features, which are the features of my mother. My sister's interpretation of her dream was accurate.

I haven't heard Jeannine refer to Cooper since that conversation. I could call her right now and ask her to verify some details but I don't want to do that. That would be unfeeling. She must think about him. She must dream of him, incessantly, relentlessly, of what he didn't become.

Perhaps she keeps his birth and death certificates in a shoebox in a closet, pulls them out occasionally when no one is home. She takes off the paper clip that keeps them together and examines the documents issued in consecutive weeks: these vital records are so similar, you can hardly tell them apart; they're yellowing at the same pace, though she notices the birth certificate is slightly yellower.

And, every now and then, she slips away from work at the library and visits Cooper's grave at the Fremantle Cemetery.

Jeannine knows the way to his grave like the palm of her hand. She stands there graveside and wonders what her son is up to. She stares at the headstone, which is already weathered; reading those dates of his birth and his death, as close together as the shoulders of the pall-bearers, she feels like she's regarding one of those old graves in the cemetery, from the nineteenth century, when babies were always dying early.

I've gone to the cemetery's website to locate his grave, but it produces no results. I've thought about that grave's *compact dimensions*. In theoretical physics there is a theory of the same name: *A compact dimension is curled up in itself and very small. Anything moving along this dimension's direction would return to its starting point, almost instantaneously. The dimension is smaller than the smallest particle and cannot be observed by conventional means.*

I don't understand this theory, and *Wikipedia* claims *the article cites no sources and can therefore be challenged and removed*, but I know it pertains to Cooper, *curled up in himself, and so small.*

Cooper's death—all death—remains an abstraction, but all abstractions, no matter how mysterious, turn into sorrow. Do you think my sister cries by his grave or does she know that the dead have no time or patience for our tears? She must talk to him. Talk more frankly than she does to her three boys. There are no transcripts of these conversations, but I reckon she's like me, she believes life gets in the way of real intimacy; it's only in death that you can get to know someone.

Maybe my sister is more connected to Cooper than her other sons.

And maybe she still sees him. That night on the porch, Paul went inside to get some food and Jeannine whispered, "Do you want to know something?"

"Sure," I said.

Before confiding in me, my sister, whom I resemble more than any of my other siblings, made me promise not to tell a living soul. I think it's okay to tell you. You seem like a person who's pretty good at keeping secrets.

"I can feel him around the house," she said, looking around and then looking into the night. "Especially on the porch. I've even see him a few times out here; he gives off this blue glow, and I try to hold him, comfort him, but he won't let me, or it's not physically possible, because how can you hold, grasp something ungraspable?"

A Hole in the Ground

If the cycle of experience is correct, then you and I are already disintegrating.

I used to think coffins were placed directly in the dirt. That's how they show it in the movies.

But one time I was walking at Holy Cross, in the Our Lady of Peace section, when I came upon a gray concrete container. I found out its proper name later, a *burial vault*, or *grave liner*. That's what they put the actual coffin inside.

According to the cemetery's glossary, *These sealed units are engineered to support the weight of the earth above the coffin and the movement of heavy maintenance equipment, to prevent the coffin from sinking too far down.*

The vault I saw was plain, like a coffin's exoskeleton, *2,600 pounds of pure concrete*, but Holy Cross sells fancier ones with names like *Divine Savior* and *Divine Mercy* and the less hopeful *Gethsemane*, which are as flashy as the coffins themselves. Though who's there to appreciate the design, apart from the creepy-crawlies that are mainly blind, more intent on wriggling their way into the container and into our orifices?

A grave liner's purpose is not aesthetic but functional: To defer decay, to protect the sanctity of the coffin and the virtue of the corpse, and to keep the ground even, so mourners don't twist their ankles. To repress and conceal the fact that a cemetery is a space made up of holes.

I used to think a *plot* and a *grave* were the same thing, as commutable as dark-haired identical twins. But as the glossary also informed me, *A plot*

131

is the measured piece of land in a cemetery purchased to obtain burial rights, and generally contains two or more graves, which are essentially excavations in the earth.

If I were to put this in my own words, a grave is a cavity formed in the plot, which is the ground for the dead body's secret plan.

Another time, I was walking in the Our Lady of Perpetual Help section, and I was so preoccupied I walked right up to the lip of one of these *excavations.* There was no one around, no gravedigger with his shovel or whatever machinery they use to dig graves. They hadn't put up a sign or any of that caution tape. I nearly fell in. I could have broken my leg. Or my neck.

It's like that grave was waiting for me. And once you're in a grave, I bet it's hard to get out. You might not want to get out of your very own hole, your hollow, your indentation.

Maybe I should just stick to the cemetery's glossary. It's safer and more instructive, offers up meaning more readily. All those graves at Holy Cross are way too real, but they're also knockoffs, cheap imitations. Graves are not only receptacles for storing bodies; they're substitutes for the lack of an actual hole. They're holes of an artificial nature. In the absence of a metaphysical hole through which we might reach the secret of death, we must get by with these man-made holes.

Still, it's good to get outside and stretch your legs.

Odors

*So tell me, what does a dead body smell like? I mean, really
smell like?*

On the Internet, that bottomless hole that has a stench of its own,
due to all the decomposing, scattered scraps of incompletely oxidized
information, there are chat rooms dedicated to this question. It seems
like everyone is dwelling on and deliberating over the particularly foul-
smelling fifth stage of death, *putrefaction*, a term that derives from the
Latin *putrere*, to be rotten, *putere*, to stink, and *facere*, to perform, to
suffer, to make, do; everyone wants to know about the olfactory component of the procedure, that future pastime in which we ooze into goo
and dissolve.

People offer various answers to evoke the dead's redolence—*rank
and sweet, like rotting meat and cheap perfume*—but my favorite response
is *a decomposing body smells like nothing else in this world.*

At school I was taught by nuns who smelled like nuns that Saint Bernadette's incorruptible corpse emitted the scent of roses. *When I was in
Nevers,* Sister Agatha told us, *paying adoration at her open crystal coffin, I
put my nose right up to her face, and the bouquet of her corpse was more
beautiful than any rose garden.* When Sister Agatha came near your desk,
you had to hold your breath; her habit held the aroma of the vapor from
the stagnant water in her hot steam iron.

A recent story from the California section of the *Los Angeles Times* related
an incident in San Clemente, in which an entire family was found dead

in their house with an ocean view. The family members, all of whom were lying on their beds, dressed in black, had been deceased for just over two weeks. A suicide pact; the note left no explanation. *Due to the unpleasant fumes,* the police had to wear underwater breathing apparatus, *as if they were going deep-sea diving.*

What does someone who's been resurrected smell like? I like that moment in the story of Lazarus when Martha warns Jesus *that there will be an odor, for he has been dead four days.* But Jesus ignores her and goes into the tomb; he doesn't seem to fear or mind the odor of death. Out comes Lazarus, wrapped in his dirty, fetorous bandages.

To thank Jesus, Martha and Mary have him over for supper. Lazarus is there. He's weirdly quiet. Mary anoints Jesus's feet with some ointment; *the house is filled with the fragrance.* If you read between the lines, this gesture can be seen not merely as one of respect, but serving a practical purpose, motivated by the presence of their recently dead brother. You sense that beneath the sweet fragrance everyone can still catch a whiff of Lazarus, who must reek of the void.

On the Internet there are fragrance-free images of bodies in service to putrefaction. If I can't inhale their aromas, I will not look at them. If there is a central tenet or organizing principle to the system I've cobbled together, it's that the dead are perfect, their bodies quietly rotting away behind their immaculate reflection.

I was taught by priests with whisky on their breath that hell stinks to high heaven, but Heaven itself is odorless. The same goes for Holy Cross, where there is a distinct absence of odors. There are no noxious fumes or vile gases. In this sense, the cemetery is successful. All I've ever detected there is the faintly bitter scent coming from my own body, the indescribable aroma of your body, and the clean scent of freshly cut grass.

Aino's Song

Verse:
A name is a strange and twisted thing.
It will outlast you.
After you're gone, your name will go on happily without you.
Chorus:
There is no avoiding my name.

My name is Ay-no Paa-so-nen.

That's how Aino introduced herself at our boring faculty meetings. She cut quite a figure at these. As we went around the table, most of us would just say our names and what we taught, but Aino would put on a small production.

She would pronounce her name emphatically, the syllables spaced apart, like a language instruction tape. *It's Finnish,* she'd tell us. *I teach literature and translation,* she'd say.

Then she would proceed to recount her life story.

And I would proceed to space out. I'd look out the window, to see if anything was going on in the cemetery.

I know we spoke at these quarterly meetings and when we ran into each other in the halls, coming to and from class, but it should come as no surprise that I wasn't particularly aware of Aino until I found out she was dying. That's when I stopped staring out the window and began to observe her.

Aino had short brown hair that was parted on the side, dark-brown
eyes, and pale skin. She wore these skirt suits that were both stylish yet
outdated, démodé, like the suits Jackie Kennedy wore, without the
timeless quality. Aino didn't wear makeup except for a streak of bright-
red lipstick.

There was an anachronistic aspect to her appearance. When I first
caught sight of her, five or so years ago, she would have been around
sixty, but her demeanor was youthful; with that schoolboy's haircut and
an androgynous face, she resembled a teenage boy playing dress-up in
his mother's clothes.

And of course there were those lengthy, otherworldly introductions:
from what I could gather, Aino was born somewhere in Europe during World War II—1943, I think, though I never figured out where
precisely—*in the cradle of Fascism, amid the bombed-out ruins*, her
words. When she was a child, her family moved from country to country,
from Hungary to Sweden to Italy to France, *hopping around like birds,
eating scraps, developing an ear for languages along the way*. When her
family sailed to America, she wandered the decks, from first class down
to steerage, *listening to other immigrants gossiping in their mother tongues*.

Aino spoke fifteen or sixteen languages in all, not counting Middle
High German and some arcane Finnish dialects. Her academic area of
specialty was Greek antiquity—those formative years in postwar Europe
gave her *an affinity for ruins*—along with Italian literature. I know she
taught Dante and took her students to the Getty to see the Renaissance
portraits, *so they can behold the faces that captivated Dante, so they can
look upon the face of Beatrice Portinari and be equally besotted*. Aino
seemed to be working on about a thousand writing projects at any given
time: translations of Italian Renaissance poetry and *a number of significant
Finnish poets* and then there was her memoir, which, from what I could
gather, was *a book of memories of my rootless childhood: an entire life not
knowing which tongue was my mother*, her words.

What struck me most about Aino, far more than her appearance or her preambles, was her . . . warmth, this feeling of boundless . . . generosity she emanated and that I didn't return.

I first learned that Aino was unwell at a meeting, though not from her; she wasn't there. She was meant to be, but as Herta, the chair of the BA program, explained, Aino was in Philadelphia and had been rushed to a hospital. Details were scarce: all Herta knew was Aino had lost consciousness and they had to perform emergency surgery. Apparently Aino was doing alright; her condition was stable.

Without Aino, preliminaries were short and to the point, and we moved quickly through all the tedious items of agenda.

A couple of months later, Aino was back, dressed in a skirt suit—this one was tweed, like the kind Miss Marple wears in Agatha Christie mysteries. Aino had a big white bandage wrapped around her head. When it came her turn to speak, she announced her name and told us what happened.

"Well," she said, with her usual ardor, "I've been on quite an adventure lately." She described the circumstances: She had flown to Philadelphia to look after her mother, who was in her early nineties and whose health was ailing. Her mom had a procedure and Aino was set to return to LA. But on the way to the airport, she had blacked out in the cab and had to be taken back to the same hospital her mother was in.

"It turns out I had a brain tumor," Aino said, "the size of an orange, a small orange. They operated on me immediately."

"So far so good," she said, when someone asked how the operation had gone. "I'm on my first course of chemotherapy and the doctors are optimistic."

Aino's refined face was swollen from the drugs and the violence of the operation, but she was beaming, like she had won a prize.

"I'm learning so much about the brain. All this wonderful knowledge. When they split open my skull and removed the tumor, I felt like I'd given birth to something, like Athena sprung from the head of Zeus. Afterward they showed me X-rays; where they had taken out the tumor there was a huge crater. It was as though I had landed on the surface of the moon." She laughed.

"And I was struck by how kind people were. When I first got to the hospital, I woke up for a while. Because it was all so sudden, I hadn't dressed properly and I was cold, and a nurse gave me her cardigan and said I could keep it. I've been wearing it ever since." She opened up the flap of her jacket to show us the olive green wool. "It's my good luck charm."

Aino was around quite a bit after that.

She appeared to be her buoyant self, but I began to detect a . . . change in her personality.

It was a little hard to tell at first: she had always been extravagant when she talked, overexcited as she ran through her stream of enthusiasms. Initially, it was as if she had just . . . turned up the volume on her persona a notch or two, become a more heightened version of herself.

She resumed her regular opening remarks, though when she said her name, she pronounced it even more dramatically, extending each syllable, slowing her name down, as if she were trying to prolong the sound of her name.

Her intros themselves kept getting more protracted, full of digressions, sort of . . . ragged around the edges. Aino would talk of her early childhood, but she would linger in the past, weave in tiny, disjointed memories of *eating a pastry on the Boulevard Haussmann or petting a goat in a village in Italy or watching the fish swim beneath a frozen lake in Sweden.*

"And the fumes," she said once, referring to the odor of the bombed European cities she and her family wandered through. "That's the smell of my childhood. It escorted us everywhere, even to America. I can still smell those fumes."

This reverie led Aino to another, less-distant anecdote, about an artist's colony she had lived at in Malibu, Positano, I think it was called, *a bohemian pastoral paradise*, but Aino told us the colony was destroyed in a fire. "I lost everything," she said. "And losing everything was a kind of revelation."

There was more to it, Aino said . . . so much more, but as she rambled on, my mind wandered in and out of what she was saying. Some days I would resume my old habits and tune out completely; the magnetic pull of the cemetery was simply too strong.

There was one day when Aino had my complete focus. Do you know how rare that is?

She was telling us about a book, not one she was writing but a book she had published, about an Italian author, Alessandro Manzoni.

I have no idea how she even got onto this, but she was trying to elucidate her theory of *the figura of the hourglass* in his novel *The Betrothed*. Something about *the figura of the hourglass as a metaphysical interpretation of the nature of life, which, in Catholic eschatology, must pass through death, in order to enter into another form of life, an afterlife which is . . . eternal.*

I can't say that those were her exact words. What I can tell you is that, as she talked, giving us her impromptu lecture, which, in its attempt to clarify her thesis, only served to make it more opaque, Aino pulled something out of the pocket of this big black trench coat she had taken to wearing, over her other layers, *to stay warm.* I couldn't make out the object, it was so small, but then I saw it was an hourglass, the size of a hummingbird; she had brought one with her to illustrate her point, like it was show-and-tell.

She made no reference to it, but, as she kept talking, droning on and on about *Manzoni and figuras and hourglasses and the symphonic, centrifugal movement between life and death*, and *how life is lined with time, like a coat is lined with silk*, she played with the small object, which was the most exquisite thing I've ever seen, turning it up and down in the palm of her hand.

Not content to stop there, Aino switched gears and began discussing the translations she was working on, simultaneously, *in a frenzy*. She recited a poem, line by line, a verse in Finnish, then in English, though she kept correcting herself, doubting her translation, rectifying her word choice: she gave up on the poem midstanza and moved on to the subject of her memoir.

"But I use the term *memoir* cautiously, because the book is not strictly nonfiction," she said, still turning the hourglass in her hand. "I imagine what my life might have been like if the war didn't happen, if I grew up in Finland, instead of nomadically, translinguistically, switching languages and landscapes until my identity itself was open to question. In the book, I slip in words in multifarious tongues, untranslated, so the reader will have the same disorienting experience I had as a girl. I've been writing this book all my life. It's all in here," she said, tapping her forehead with her free hand. "And it's nearly finished. I just have to fiddle with the end, which is eluding me, but I'll finish it as soon as I get the time because there's this other book I'm eager to start . . ."

People in the room were getting annoyed, or perhaps that was just me. The dying are a source of vexation; they are visible symbols of what's in store for us. Aino had acquired some of the dead's irritating habits, their disdain for order and propriety.

Herta jumped in and thanked Aino and patted her gently on the shoulder. Aino smiled and looked baffled. She put the hourglass down on the table. I don't think she knew how long she had been talking. It was as if she was beginning to lose a sense of time, or had already entered a space where time had a new value, no value, a useless currency.

But then she looked embarrassed. She blushed, red against the faded blackness of her trench coat.

What with all her babbling, Aino started to seem like a crazy woman, and she looked the part, in that trench coat, with her bandaged head. Her face remained puffy, like a child with mumps, but she was perpetually smiling like a demented man in the moon.

I stayed clear of the weird lady with the hole in her skull. I made sure I didn't sit near Aino, and if I saw her at the end of the hall, I would act like I didn't see her and walk the other way. I didn't want to get caught in an interminable conversation that would be tricky to extricate myself from, and I didn't want to get too . . . close to her. Physically, I mean. She kind of . . . repulsed me.

Even from a safe distance, Aino's bandages reeked, her green cardigan too—one time she told us she never washed it, *so the cardigan would retain its talismanic charm.*

Can't animals smell when another animal is dying and then keep well away? From a certain perspective, I was an unfeeling human, but from another viewpoint I was merely acting like an ordinary animal.

It became obvious that death was altering Aino, inside and out, yet I thought she was going to be okay. She hardly ever acknowledged her illness, and if she did, she was upbeat, dismissing it with a wave of her hand: *there are all these new technologies and the drugs are doing wonders.* I believed Aino would just go on being ill . . . indefinitely. But then suddenly she wasn't at any of the meetings and had to cancel her classes, and I didn't have to avoid her anymore.

One afternoon I was leaving class when I saw a former student of Aino's, Gleah, who has red hair that stands on end, like she has thrust her finger in an electric socket. Gleah was also my student, though I feel uncomfortable using that phrase, *my student,* in that it implies I was her teacher and therefore must have taught her something.

We began to chat, in this narrow space wedged between two classrooms, located near an emergency exit. Gleah told me she had graduated and was at the university on some financial business.

I feigned interest until I figured I could inquire about Aino. I knew they were friends; Gleah lived around the corner from Aino in West LA. She said that Aino had another tumor—or was it that the tumor had come back? This one was much smaller than the first—Aino,

Gleah said, had likened it to the size of a cherry—but it was infinitely more dangerous, in a region of the brain that controls all thought and speech.

So that's why Aino's spiels were so free-associative; it had nothing to do with eccentricity or exuberance: the cherry-sized tumor must have been putting pressure on her brain, so her thoughts spilled out uncontrollably.

Gleah had been driving Aino to the university, until she stopped teaching, chauffeuring her around. She had even taken her to the hospital.

"The tumor is basically inoperable," Gleah said, "but she's been getting some last-option treatment at Cedars Sinai. I spent a whole day with her, in the basement. You wouldn't believe what they do down there." Gleah has pale-blue eyes and they opened really wide.

"The door was open briefly so I got a quick look. They had Aino strapped into this metal apparatus, like some medieval torture device, straight out of the Inquisition. Her head was locked into it with these big metal clamps so she couldn't move. And then they flooded her brain with ridiculous amounts of radiation, for two or three hours; it was like they were bombing her brain, nuking it. Even though it isn't even going to fucking help."

Gleah was getting more and more worked up as she talked. She's the kind of person who emotes, is quick to anger; I can only achieve this in dreams. I didn't want to look at her face, so I stared at her hair, as red and bright as the handle on the glass emergency exit door; she must have dyed it recently.

"It made me so damn furious," she said. "It was this experimental treatment, a research project, more for the doctors than Aino, and the doctors wouldn't tell us anything. When they were done, I asked Aino how she felt and she told me it was like being struck by lightning, but in your brain. You know Aino; she said something about Zeus playing with his lightning bolts in her mind. Though she could scarcely speak. When I drove her home she just kind of . . . collapsed in the back seat."

Gleah stopped talking. I looked quickly at her face and saw her blue eyes were watering, deep pools, so I returned my gaze to her hair.

"That was awhile ago. I hadn't heard from Aino and it was kind of a relief. I thought I should check in, so I called and Aino's brother picked up. He said that Aino couldn't come to the phone but would love to see me. The last I heard, Aino and her brother hadn't talked in years. I should drop in. When someone's ill and their estranged brother visits, it can't mean anything good."

Gleah had been a useful source of information, but she wasn't the one who eventually notified me of Aino's death. That came in a group e-mail from human resources.

I stopped whatever it was that I was doing—the event of Aino's death suspended the monotony of my work day—and read the subject heading: *The Passing of a Dear Colleague.*

I suppose it's a good thing, letting everyone at the university know, but it chilled me, the idea of having your death relayed in a memo, by human resources, circulated and blind-copied in an electronic communication you're unable to open.

As I sat at my computer and skimmed that bureaucratic document, which gave a more reliable summary of Aino's life than the one I gave you, I thought back to those meetings, Aino's meandering monologues, especially during her later, most manic phase, and I understood her logic, which went beyond the neurological effects of the tumor: every time she told us her biography—expanding it, repeating it, revising it, deforming it—she did so with the knowledge that she was a woman preparing her own obituary.

And then a memory rose in me, something I had forgotten. When people die, flow out of the world, a certain pressure can be relieved, through an almost hydraulic mechanism, releasing memories.

Aino had come to a reading I did at the university, a few years ago, when my book came out. Did I tell you I wrote a book, a book of all my obsessions? It doesn't matter; you wouldn't have heard of it. Anyway, I noticed her during the reading, sitting in the first row with this blank look on her face.

Afterward, she bought a copy and I signed it, but when I handed the book back to her with my freshly inscribed name, her mien was inscrutable; she didn't say anything, or offer any words of congratulation. This was unlike Aino, normally so vocal in her praise. I was a little put out at the time.

Now that Aino was gone, I could see the look on her face more clearly than before, when she was right in front of me, her expression that was a kind of ghost, as all expressions are, in that they are invisible yet promote the movement of the facial muscles, to convey an identifiable emotion, or lack thereof. Only now was I able to interpret her silence; I shouldn't have taken it so personally. It was the blankness of the dead that Aino displayed that night, their reserve, their reticence.

I had to meet with Herta that day. I walked upstairs to her office. She had taped a photo of Aino on her door. Aino looked very young: long dark glossy hair, pale skin, a real beauty—vaguely reminiscent of the woman I knew.

"Yes, she was a total knockout," Herta said when I commented on the picture.

We were meant to discuss a work-related matter, *there were some issues regarding my performance*, but we ended up talking about Aino. Herta had visited her a couple of weeks before she died.

"Aino couldn't really see by then," Herta told me, in her usual careful tone, "but she seemed to know who I was by the sound of my voice. She asked how things were at the university. 'I'll be back next quarter,' she said. 'What do you want me to teach?' At times she spoke as if she were going to recover, but at other times she was lucid, more . . . cognizant of her predicament. She said some students had dropped in and she gave them a brief lesson on death. 'What better place to teach than from your deathbed?' she said. She taught them the various words for death, and she started to recite the list for me, *Halal, Mavet, Mort, Morte, Mors, Muerte, Smrt, Thanatos, Tod,* oh, and *Kuolema,* the Finnish word for death . . . those are just a few. Aino had me write the words down and repeat them out loud like I was one of her students, which I suppose I was. When I was done, she gestured for me to come near her and she whispered in my ear, 'You know the number of words for death is infinite . . .'"

I asked Herta what else Aino had told her about death, taught her, but Herta didn't answer my question. She looked at me as if she was considering it, then moved on. She said their conversation was interrupted by a phone call. Aino's friend Juliette had called from Paris, and Aino's brother got her on the phone.

"It was incredible," Herta said, "to hear this woman, who was in such a poor physical state, talk so gaily and quickly in French. Aino was chatting and laughing as if she were at a cocktail party. They spoke for quite a while, and when it came time to say good-bye, Aino kept saying 'Merci, merci, amis pour toujours, amis pour toujours . . .'

"But she had tired herself out." Herta paused, like she was getting tired as well. She was wearing a dark suit, and I gazed at the fabric's pinstripes, so fine as to be indiscernible.

"After she got off the phone," Herta said, "Aino seemed to be in this whole other realm, floating somewhere between West LA and Paris. She would say something tangential and translate it, not just into one language but into all those languages she knew. I think she was striving to keep her brain active, to keep practicing what she had learnt throughout her life, so she wouldn't lose her skills. It was like being at the United Nations and hearing each statement translated over headphones into multiple tongues.

"And the register of her voice kept changing. Sometimes it was quite deep and then it would become very high and childlike. She kept shifting registers, never speaking in a register that was her own. Watching the words come out of Aino's lips, which were cracked and covered in sores, was uncanny, like watching one of those old European movies that have been dubbed into English. I stopped talking and just sat there and listened to Aino and all her voices until it was time for me to say good-bye.

"When I did, I told Aino that I was thinking of her. Although her eyes were clouded with cataracts, they seemed to focus, and she looked at me, even though she couldn't see me. She smiled and said, 'Don't worry, everything is fine, all is well, everything is fine.' She kept smiling and repeating this statement, over and over. The way she was projecting her voice and its cadence reminded me of those town criers who used to wander around villages in the medieval period, making public announcements. But the voice also seemed to . . . stream from her depths. She was virtually . . . singing her . . . proclamation, in this unearthly voice, like the Sirens . . ."

Herta had begun to speak quickly, and excitably, which was out of character, as if, like Aino, she was also channeling an alien register. As if she were channeling Aino. Or speaking from some new depths that had opened up inside of her. Ordinarily, Herta keeps herself together; she has this Germanic cool: her face and her pale-blue eyes tend to be expressionless.

She was still composed, but there was something tumultuous beneath her surface: nothing as blatant as Gleah's show of emotion, just a flickering in her eyes. Herta grew silent, as if she were listening to Aino's voice, as if she could still hear the voice that rose from Aino's depths, the voice that wasn't Aino at all, or, conversely, was truly Aino, her real voice, the voice that is only released in death. I could see that Herta had been taken off course by Aino's song, like Ulysses and his crew, and she would have been better off not listening, plugging her ears with wax.

She appeared to have forgotten I was there, but as I made to leave, Herta added, "I won't forget that voice for a long, long time."

There was a memorial for Aino, but I didn't go. It would have involved taking three buses.

Though I did have a dream about her memorial, so I did attend, in a way.

The dream took place in a church. Someone was giving a eulogy, but I couldn't hear or see properly—the space was dimly lit and I was sitting in a pew near the back—so I moved to a pew near the front. Aino herself was eulogizing—somehow, aware that she was the guest of honor, she had circumvented the absence requirement of a memorial.

She looked handsome, austere: her hair was slicked back, her face pale, though she still wore lipstick. She was dressed in black trousers and a black shirt. The shirt's fabric was glossy, just like a shirt I had as a teenager and misplaced. How did Aino get a hold of my shirt? Just like Mussolini's Blackshirts—the fascism of death, I thought, a centralizing network that rules every movement of life.

Aino was standing behind a lectern, with a massive Bible spread open in front of her: *Turn to Genesis, cage number 93*, she said, instead of *page number 93*—the tumor must still be pressing on her brain, distorting her speech in death, I thought.

I tried to listen but I was distracted: without leaving the pulpit, Aino changed outfits, like actresses change their gowns when they're hosting the Academy Awards. She was now wearing a knitted pink Giorgio Armani skirt suit from the 1970s, shot through with silver thread. I knew she was relaying her message from the dead, that every word was of great importance, but my eyes were dazzled by the silver-pink fabric glittering in the half dark and I missed most of her eulogy—which rhetorically was more of a sermon—except for these lines: *Dying can be considered an act of translation in which we are converted from one form into another medium that is . . . unintelligible. The problem of death is the problem of translation, the problem of death . . .*

Aino had not finished, I knew that she would never finish, but I had to be elsewhere, life I suppose . . .

Aino once compared her brain tumor to an exotic orchid blooming in a greenhouse; however, deaths are not unique, and brain tumors are run of the mill, in the scheme of things.

Yet the circumstances of her fate are worth noting. Aino loved nothing more than the life of the mind, and, alert to this, Death went straight for her brain, the organ she most cherished, just as he would go for the voice box of an opera singer or the prick of a Don Juan. Death knows where to strike.

Though perhaps he or it bears us no spite. Aino's ninety-three-year-old mother outlived her daughter; she was alive at the time of Aino's death. Aino flew to see her mother, expecting her to die, but when she landed in Philadelphia, they . . . swapped fates. Or Death got confused, mistook daughter for mother. Death made . . . a mistake.

That book Aino was working on, her memoir, the one that was as good as done—apparently, no one can find any record of it: no file, no hard copy, not even notes.

From what Herta and Gleah told me, there are conflicting theories going around, depending on whom you talk to.

Some friends claim that Aino finished the book, not long before she died, but she hid the manuscript and forgot where she put it.

Others are of the opinion that the book existed once, long ago, but was lost in the fire in Malibu, and Aino, heartbroken, could never bring herself to rewrite it.

A few cynics say that Aino never wrote a word of this memoir; it was something she planned to do, when she had time. The only place the book existed was in the gray folds of her brain.

I can't settle on any one theory; they all sound plausible. I've even come up with some of my own, like maybe the book did go up in smoke, not in the blaze at Positano, *in which all 113 of the colony's horses were burned alive*, but a more concentrated, more recent conflagration, a fire that Aino started: Aino set the book alight, as an offering, a sacrifice, hoping that in exchange for destroying her memoir, the gods would grant her life.

Or, Aino did indeed hide the book. In the delirium of illness, she appeared to have forgotten where her hiding place was, but she was being crafty, disingenuous; this was one of her more lucid moments.

She knew perfectly where she had placed the manuscript but decided, after much thought—all there is to do on a deathbed is think, die, and think—that she didn't want anyone to read the book, not if she wasn't around. With the grave clarity of the individual who is not long for this world, she concluded that people reading your book after your death is equivalent to someone gawking at your corpse, poking it with a stick. So she smiled and played dumb, like a little girl who doesn't want to share her secrets with anyone.

According to the university website, which is yet to take Aino's biography down, *she continues to work on her memoir.* Occasionally, as I walk the hallways, Aino's name pops into my head. And the thought, which is another kind of ghost, produces her apparition, a mental projection of her image. If I ran into her ghost for real, most likely I would act like I didn't see her and walk the other way. But if I gathered my courage, I could ask her about the book: where is it? Is it anywhere? I could inquire as to how her work is going in the afterlife—not writing her life story, forget life—but translating that most forked and foreign of tongues, the most difficult language to learn, the language of death; translating death, or attempting to.

How to Dispose of Me

The management desires to serve you and welcomes your suggestions. If you encounter any problems concerning your plot, please report them to our office for immediate assistance.

I don't want to be buried at Holy Cross. Perhaps when you close your eyes, it looks just like Pere Lachaise. But I would prefer to be interred in a prettier cemetery, one with upright headstones and crumbly statues that lovers can use to their advantage; a cemetery with shade-giving trees that people can lean against and dream beneath.

I don't want to be cremated: the very idea of that journey down the conveyor belt in a flimsy casket, that little black curtain you vanish behind, and *the special furnace*, subjecting your corpse to a heat of 2,000 to 2,500 degrees Fahrenheit, sends an involuntary shiver down my spine. Catholics used to forbid *this act in which a corpse is destroyed by fire*, believing cremation destroyed evidence of the soul, like shredding a document that was proof of a crime.

Eventually they relented, but I haven't; why be so eager to embrace nothingness? Surely every last vestige of individuality is lost in the furnace—though forensic experts were able to identify the boy from UCLA, mingled with all the other boys, thanks to DNA, and they say the shape of his bone fragments was unique, his ash softer than the others.

Whatever, I would rather take my time disintegrating.

150

Burial has always seemed the most attractive of options, mainly by default. Though lately, doubts have crept in, specifically around the question of cognizance and duration, and I'm not certain I want to be buried at all.

I've read up on the state's burial requirements, which are clearly defined and full of persuasive phrases like *double depth* and *undisturbed earth*. I don't have a head for dimensions; I'm more interested in the immeasurable aspects of death, but one stipulation I have retained is they seal you in real tightly at a depth of no less than four feet.

The desire is for something called *a leak-proof interment*. The primary concern is hygiene. The state seeks to prevent emissions from the corpse—scum, effluent, sludge—leaking out of the coffin into the ground above; to inhibit the dead from flowing into the water table, so we're not drinking them in the morning, getting fetid particles stuck in our teeth. The objective of the California Cemetery and Funeral Bureau is to contain the deceased, but I think the latter party might feel differently about this. The dead might be itching to escape, so they can share their discharges with us.

And what if the authorities get it wrong? Like that woman in Boyle Heights, *who was pronounced dead and placed in a body bag in a morgue drawer*. A couple of days later, when a worker opened the drawer, *the bag was partially unzipped; it appeared the woman had woken up and tried to get out*, but a body bag is not as user friendly as a sleeping bag, and she had frozen to death. They keep those morgue drawers cold, like butchers' walk-in freezers where satiny pink carcasses hang in rows on hooks.

I could get one of those safety coffins that were popular in the nineteenth century: they had a little rope inside that you could pull if you came to; this would activate a bell aboveground that would alert a night watchman. In one diagram I found, this rope is dangling by "the corpse's" hand, just in case the fingers start twitching; the rope is red, like the cord on my childhood dressing gown. I'm not sure they make these coffins anymore; there were a number of manufacturing issues. And if I were able to purchase one, what if my night watchman was sleeping or drunk or seducing another night watchman when I rang the bell?

There must be a form of compromise. I like the way they handle it on Mouth Athos, the all-male monastery on an isolated rocky island in Greece. When a monk dies, they bury him for a couple of years, in the earth, sans coffin, then exhume his bones. Dressed in their black robes and their black pillbox hats, the monks wash the skeleton in red wine, separate the 206 bones—writing the name and date of death on the skull—and then place the bones with the bones of all the other dead monks in their ossuary: skulls with skulls, ribcages with ribcages, leg bones with leg bones. So even if you or your cells are aware after death, your skeleton knows there is something to look forward to; soon you will be disinterred and disassembled and have thousands of other drunk bones to keep you company.

I'm still figuring it out, but whatever you do, don't preserve me. I don't want to be one of those shriveled pharaohs, whose organs were pickled, whose brains were yanked out of their nostrils with a long, sharp hook, doomed to be ogled in museums for centuries by schoolboys who drip snot on the glass display case.

I don't care to be laid out like Lenin in his glass coffin in his mausoleum. Dressed in an olive-green suit, with his receding hairline, pale dome of a forehead, sharp eyes, and pointy goatee, he still takes after himself, the way a wax figure at Madame Tussaud's favors the original human. I read they kept Lenin's genitals attached but removed everything vaguely internal; they soak him regularly in bleach and acid to erase the troublesome dark spots of mold and fungus on his skin, which match the black polka dots on his tie.

I mean, it's one thing to rush toward formlessness, but there's such a thing as being too intact.

The Mourner

You want to know my secret, how I've avoided death for so long? The kind of death that creates a hole inside you, a hole that could never be filled, not with all the landfill in the world. It's actually quite easy: keep your distance from everyone; don't get attached to anyone.

There are some things at Holy Cross that would be harder to show you.

Like the man I saw wearing a dark-blue shirt, wandering around with a bouquet of red flowers. It was clear from his posture of bent determination that he was looking for someone, but he seemed confused, like he hadn't been to Holy Cross in a while.

I tailed him as discreetly as possible, when suddenly he stopped.

He had found whoever it was he had come to visit. He knelt down next to the grave, placing those flowers gently, so as not to crush them.

I was wearing my strong glasses that day and I could see his lip was quivering, like he was overcome. Perhaps it was the anniversary of the person's death. I do not recall the date. The mourner had gray hair, but he was quite young. I wondered if the death was unexpected and he had gone prematurely gray. There are many reported cases of this happening. I wondered about the relation between this young man and the person in the ground. I noticed he was wearing his shirt inside out, though I couldn't read the label. He must have come to the cemetery in a hurry, eager to get there before it closed.

Or the shirt may have been intentional. I read once that at some funerals people wear their clothes inside out because they believe *the*

land of the dead is a place of opposites, where everything is done backward;
the afterlife is an inverted negative image of the world where everyone is
just a darker mirror image of themselves. In my estimation, that depiction
remains the most credible image of the afterlife, as well as the most
frightening.

It soon became apparent the mourner was talking to the person he
had come to . . . see. He was talking under his breath, in a register lower
than a whisper. He was talking to a person who, like me, could not hear
a word of what he was saying. For all intents and purposes, he was engaged in a one-way conversation.

We could claim that conferring with the dead is a futile and possibly
psychotic activity. Yet I think we'd be mistaken. I may have only spoken
to a corpse once, but I suspect it's the most profound exchange you can
have with another human being. In that they do not interrupt you, are
not distracted by their thoughts, the dead make the best listeners, far
better than the living. We could go so far as to say that the only worthwhile conversation we can have is with the dead, for they give you their
full and undivided attention.

Eun Kang and the Ocean

*To inscribe: to carve or impress a symbol on a surface, let's
say a door. There's the mark the Jews painted on their doors,
in the Book of Exodus, so the Destroyer would overlook them,
pass them by, but there must be another kind of mark, that
tells the Destroyer, "Hey, I'm inside, come get me, it doesn't
matter if you're early."*

I didn't know Eun Kang at all. I just read about her, over and over,
until she started to . . . talk to me.

Last year, on a Thursday night in December, Eun Kang was unwind-
ing in her house in Venice. A man came into her house. He raped her,
dragged her upstairs to the attic, raped her again, and then killed her.

Those are the basic details. I'm sure you want to know everything,
even if you think you don't, but let me tell you what I was up to a few
blocks away. It may turn out to be relevant.

I had taught that evening, and I got home a little after 10:00 p.m.
Tim was at a university residency in North . . . or was it South Dakota?
I tended to our dog's needs then tended to my own.

I don't believe I did anything special—wine, food, a shower, teeth,
TV—but I remember that it had been a long day, I was . . . exhausted,
and an inky, heavy feeling with no apparent cause had found its way
into my heart. Our dog picks up on emotions, so I hid the feeling from
her, and began to unwind, or tried to.

155

Shortly after I settled down in bed, and switched off the bedside lamp, I heard a helicopter circling over our house.

This is not infrequent in my neighborhood, but it sounded like there was more than one, two, even three, and they circled not just for ten minutes or so but for a long time, at a low altitude, hovering, rattling the windows and the tiles on the roof, as if they were musical instruments accompanying my uneasy state. The helicopters kept me from falling asleep, and just as I was getting there, their blades whirred into my dreams.

I slept restlessly.

It was like the helicopters and my nerves were at it all night.

In the morning, when I took out the dog to piss on the verge, a neighbor told me why the helicopters were so busy. But I don't chat with my neighbors—did I find out on the Internet? Whatever the means of communication through which I was apprised of Eun Kang's death, my reaction was straightforward: I was fascinated and/or horrified and I wanted to know more.

It seems Eun Kang had just finished dinner. Around 10:00 p.m., a stranger walked into her house on the 5600 block of Electric Avenue. He gained entry through a sliding door she had left open. The stranger proceeded to rape her in the kitchen, stabbing her multiple times with a knife she had just washed, along with the rest of the dishes, leaving them to dry in the drainer.

Hearing screams, a neighbor ran out. The neighbor *peered through the sliding door.* He had grabbed a flashlight and *shone it through the glass.*

The neighbor saw what was . . . materializing; he tried but failed to stop the killer as he took Eun Kang up to the attic.

In an interview, the neighbor stated, *I wish I hadn't seen it. I wish I could . . . remove what I saw from my own eyes.*

When police arrived at the scene, Eun Kang was alive in the attic and bleeding. The dishes were still drying.

She was pronounced dead at the hospital at 11:15 p.m. Her unborn child, a boy, was pronounced dead three minutes later. The autopsy report used the verb *destroyed* in reference to the death of the fetus.

Eun Kang, four months pregnant, was going to have twins. *Both feti were destroyed*—the plural of fetus is *fetuses*, not *feti*, but the report used the term ungrammatically. The second unborn child, another boy, was not *discovered*—an odd word choice, I thought, *discovered*—until a second autopsy was conducted that Friday.

The suspect was apprehended roughly three hours after the incident. He was on the beach, sleeping by the sea.

His clothes were bloodstained. You would think he would have gone into the ocean to clean his clothes. You would think it would be impossible to sleep after doing what he did, but apparently it was nearly impossible to wake him up; an arresting officer said *it was like trying to wake up a teenager in the morning.*

According to police records, the twenty-two-year-old male was a transient, a drifter: in and out of jails for a series of minor offenses, several stays in mental hospitals, *though nothing to indicate the possibility of violence.* One report characterized him somewhat unprofessionally as *a very strange young man.*

In photos taken by a courtroom photographer, this *strange young man* wears a lemon-yellow jumpsuit. On another day he wore a blue jumpsuit, lending him the appearance of a hospital orderly.

The suspect's facial expressions also changed. In some images he looks earnest while in others he seems bewildered, perhaps by the charge of *three counts of murder.*

During the arraignment, he said he *liked the sound of the fountain* in Eun Kang's garden; that's what drew him to her house. *The house seemed very peaceful.* It gave him *a good feeling.*

Because the door was open, he thought it meant *Eun Kang wanted him to come in.*

I thought I was helping her, he said, and went on to explain his theory that *every individual has an expiration date,* assigned at birth, and this date is imprinted on each individual's skin, *just like a use-by date on a bottle of milk. I can smell when people's shelf lives have expired,* he said. *Everyone's perishable. Most people can't see this expiration mark,* he said, *but I can see.*

As I read and reread the various accounts, it occurred to me that the killer walked into Eun Kang's house around the same time I walked into mine. Except I had to use a key. And that inky feeling that seeped into my heart as events unfolded on the 5600 block of Electric—was there any line of causation?

In Greek mythology there are three Fates—the spinner who spins the thread of life, the allotter who measures the thread apportioned to each individual, and the unturnable, who selects the type of death, the time of death, and cuts the thread. Eun Kang's fate was terrible on three counts.

She was also subject to the fourth Fate, the one mythology forgot about, the inscriber, the one who inscribes. To be written about posthumously. To get your picture in the papers because of the way you died; to have strangers pore over your violent death, endlessly.

You could argue it's worse to go through something like that and not be written about. *At least she's remembered,* you might say. *At least people know her name.*

Questions arose in my brain:
    What did Eun Kang eat that night?

Did she hear the intruder outside or the click of the sliding door?

How did she address the intruder when he first presented himself?

As the incident . . . developed, did Eun Kang call out to God to intervene?

Did she pray, scream, or sing a sort of combined *screamprayer*?

If she called out to God, did he answer?

What was in Eun Kang's heart as the night . . . transpired?

When she looked in the face of her killer, what did she see? and

What was her final thought?

And Eun Kang herself? Who was she?

The articles were only slightly more informative on this matter. She was thirty-nine at the time of her death, my age.

In a photo in the *Los Angeles Times'* Homicide Report, her straight black hair is pulled back from a broad face. She wears a white V-necked top and a fine gold chain; her skin is pale, her gaze . . . intense, as if her expression was preparing itself for what lay ahead. It is the photo for her driver's license, the unsmiling countenance one adopts when posing for any bureaucratic mode of identification.

Eun Kang had moved to New York from Korea when she was twenty-seven, to look after her twin brother who was dying of cancer. He died and in 2003 she came to Southern California to take over the family dry-cleaning business.

Family members *declined to comment*, apart from one distant relative who told the reporter, *we just want to forget*.

One small thing I learned about Eun Kang: she surfed. A friend of hers was interviewed and spoke of how much Eun Kang loved the sea.

The friend said something interesting. That summer, Eun Kang went surfing every day, often twice a day; *it was like she was compelled to go surfing. As if, while she still had the chance, she wanted to enjoy every wave in the ocean, every current, every tide.*

The article had a snapshot of Eun Kang, down the beach in her wetsuit, grasping her surfboard. Her black hair was tied back from her broad face, like in the other photo, but in this one she was smiling.

And in this image she looked vaguely familiar. I wondered if I had seen her that summer, when I also went to the beach virtually every day, early in the morning or late in the afternoon, eager to feel the cold water's neutralizing effect, driven by my own compulsion. It wasn't that unlikely; maybe we went to the same stretch of beach, between the pier and life-guard station #13 (where, incidentally, the killer chose to sleep.) Though at the beach, immersed in the ocean's briny, watery waste, people all look the same, their identity drained, or washed away.

I made a special trip to the deli to get a hard copy of the article, which was in one of the Venice papers. When I went to the counter to buy a couple of things, the owner saw the paper, with the picture of Eun Kang and her surfboard on the cover, and shook his head.

"What a tragic thing," he said. "You know she worked here?"

"Really?" I had been going to this deli for years, but this was the first time he had engaged me in conversation. "When was that?"

"Just a few months ago. She was a very nice lady. A tragic thing."

As he gave me my change, a picture of Eun Kang appeared in my mind. The owner is generally the only person working—a woman who seems to be his wife helps out occasionally—so I'm always aware of new faces.

And I remembered seeing a new face one day. It had to be Eun Kang.

She rang me up, as her boss stood beside her. She seemed nervous, learning the ropes of a new job. I smiled at her and she smiled at me. She returned my change, her fingerprints and DNA staining the coins and bills.

I didn't bring up this memory, but before I left the owner told me they hired Eun Kang because they thought their new sandwich business was going to be busy. It never took off; they didn't need her after all.

There was a vigil for Eun Kang. I did not consider attending—my relationship with the dead is primarily one on one, not communal—but I did pay my respects, a week or so later. On my birthday, December 27. Tim asked me what I felt like doing and I said, "Why don't we take the dog for a walk, visit Eun Kang's house?"

Birthdays set me on edge, and I guess I hoped this might make me feel a little less crazy. I had some misguided idea that viewing the house would be a good thing to do, humbling, a Zen exercise; it would put things into perspective.

I don't know what I was thinking. As we walked down Electric, along the old tram tracks, I immediately got a bad vibe. The morning was gray and damp, as damp and gray as the feeling that crept into my heart the night of Eun Kang's death.

It took us awhile to find the place—we went in the wrong direction, then noticed the numbers were getting lower, not higher. So we headed back toward Venice Boulevard, which meets Electric at a perpendicular angle.

The house at 5660 Electric Avenue was nearer to us than I had thought. Hidden behind a high bamboo fence, there wasn't much to see. Just a red-tiled roof. I could hear the gentle burbling of the fountain. I could appreciate the attraction, what drew the killer inside. If you didn't know any better, the house could seem inviting, could be mistaken for a calm and quiet space.

But there was this dense . . . energy oozing through the gaps in the bamboo fence, an energy that pervaded the whole street and hung in the air, mingling with the gray mist.

As if Eun Kang was still around, floating . . . everywhere. The papers described her as a small woman, but now that she was dead she seemed to be taking up much more space in the atmosphere.

Which makes sense. While we're alive the soul is cooped up in our bodies; unrestrained, the soul is able to suffuse as it pleases, spread itself out . . .

Or maybe I've been living in California too long and have been brainwashed by its motley array of New Age ideologies. There has to be a rational explanation: the meteorological conditions, a projection of my mood, the electric currents emanating from the wires above our heads. Electric Avenue was named after the former power station, and though the station closed, it's still the location of a central circuit. Whether the cause was logical or mystical, I turned to Tim and asked if we could get out of there.

I had seen a picture of a memorial to Eun Kang that her friends and neighbors had erected on the sidewalk outside her gate—a table laden with Buddhas, candles, notes, and flowers. The structure was gone, but as we left, I spotted a note stapled to a telephone pole:

Eun Kang, I hope you and your twins are in heaven. I hope your killer gets struck by lightning. How could a soul ever be cleansed of such evil? Your murderer is a vicious animal. I hope he gets the chair. If a bear attacks a person in a forest, they put the animal down . . .

While Tim wasn't looking, I tore off the message, a remnant from the memorial, and put it in my pocket, a birthday gift. At home I pasted it into a notebook I had bought at the deli. I had intended to use this notebook for writing, but, lacking inspiration, was instead using it to keep all my clippings about Eun Kang together, in one place.

I did my best to uncover further aspects of her story, but whenever I entered the search terms *Eun Kang Venice murder biography*, I received the same results and the word *biography* was crossed out, like this:

~~Biography~~

I was, however, taken to a link on Korean ghosts.

In Korean myth there are these specters that go by the name of *Gwisin*. After death, some people hang around for assorted reasons, particularly when someone has done them an unforgiveable wrong.

Gwisin suffer from a sense of incompletion and stay here until they have finished their work, or extracted revenge.

It struck me that Eun Kang met the main criteria for this kind of ghost.

A Gwisin's presence is traditionally announced by eerie weather or an atmospheric shift; so perhaps I did perceive something that day on Electric. I continued to entertain this idea, despite the *Wikipedia* disclaimer: *This article relies too heavily on one source and may fail to make a clear distinction between fact and fiction.*

I printed out the "Gwisin" entry and added it to my EK notebook, which I kept on my bedside table, in the hope that it might infiltrate my dreams. Did you know that *Gwisin can come to you when you're awake or asleep?*

It was Eun Kang's last night. She was living in a green clapboard house, its color faded by the sea air. She had gone to bed but she was sleeping fitfully.

The killer was in the yard, standing by the fountain, biding his time.

There wasn't just one fountain; there were all these fountains, burbling and murmuring, muttering warnings in their fountain tongue, drowning out the murderer's breathing.

It was unclear who I was in the dream: Eun Kang, the killer, or an unseen third party, silently observing.

Eun Kang was sleeping in the attic but she kept waking up like she knew something or someone was outside. She went downstairs to the kitchen to get a glass of water. She thought she saw a man's blurry face through a pane of glass in the door. She assumed it was nothing but her imagination, and she went back to bed and fell back to sleep and the killer decided that it was time to come in.

On another occasion, only *he* turned up:

I was out on the street, it was *that* Thursday night, and I was just getting home from work when *he* ran past. I was startled and he stopped and looked at me and smiled. Even in the dark, I could see he had a beautiful smile.

"Sorry," he said.

"That's okay," I said. He was covered in blood; it glowed.

"Oh yeah," he said, sheepishly, brushing himself. "I just killed someone. I think you know her. Hey, can you tell me how to get from here to the beach?"

These dreams were unsettling, but I'm used to dreams, their effect. I would immediately turn on my bedside lamp and write everything down, so I wouldn't forget. Then something else happened, which I also recorded, but that's more difficult to explain.

One night I was asleep when I woke up to the sound of my own voice.

Sometimes I talk in my sleep, so loud that I wake myself up; it's no big deal. *Dying is simply a process of being unborn*, my voice said, as if it were separate from me. Intrigued by the phrase, I didn't bother to turn on the lamp, just scribbled it in the dark and was about to close my notebook when I heard a voice again: *Better to be unnamed*, the voice said.

Note that I do not say *my* voice, but *a* voice, *the* voice. To be precise I should say *her* voice, for this time the voice bore no resemblance to mine; it sounded like a female voice.

Even so, I didn't think much of it. I attributed the sensation to being overworked, overtired. I must be half-asleep, I thought.

A few nights later, I was roused by a voice that was not my own: *The relationship between the living and the dead is not fixed or reciprocal*, the voice said, *it is . . . unstable.*

This was not particularly unusual: in the past my sleep had been disrupted by the harsh sound of someone else's voice, and I could never tell where the voice was coming from, if it was a neighbor screaming outside or a persona screaming in a dream inside my head.

What was unusual was the fact that this voice was very similar to the woman's voice from a few nights before.

It's no big deal, I thought. I mean, everyone hears voices occasionally, don't they?

Over the following weeks, I heard her voice intermittently.

At first she spoke only in abstract fragments, terse utterances— *Death is a mode of nonidentification* is another of the weird things she said—and I only heard her in my sleep or right after waking, when I was drowsy.

Then one night she told me . . . not so much a story, but a sliver, a shard of a story, and I could not blame it on dreams or sleeplessness for I was sitting up in bed, reading; the lamp was on and I was wide awake:

You know I hated that goddamn dry-cleaning business, she said. *Those garment bags hanging all around me like body bags. Those tickets with their malevolent numbers and the smell of the chemical solvents. I would head to the ocean to escape the fumes . . .*

The derogatory term *woo woo* can be applied to a naïve individual who is all too willing to believe in paranormal or pseudoscientific phenomena. Was this Eun Kang communicating with me? Or was it just another auditory hallucination?

After that, *she,* whoever *she* was, only spoke to me before sleep, when the light was on. Without my asking, she began to address those concerns of mine that none of the articles were able to answer:

So you want to know what I ate for my last meal? she said. *Salmon. Wild. Caught from the Pacific. I wouldn't say I enjoyed it. Its flavor was distinctly briny. When my killer stabbed me with the knife I had used to gut the fish, its odor flowed from the holes in me, and he screwed up his face. The poor doctors smelled it too when they opened me up later, like they had walked into some hidden sea cave. God, I made such a stink!*

I wish I could say the bedroom was filled with the stench of rotten fish, but that would be untrue. All I can say is I started to feel like I knew things I shouldn't know. I started to wonder, maybe even believe, that these words weren't just coming from some unreliable place inside me but flowing directly, verbatim, in an act of dictation from the mouth of the ghost of Eun Kang herself.

Wikipedia tells us that *Gwisin have droopy black hair and their skin is transparent. They are often legless and can even be faceless, depending on their personality.*

I have to confess I never saw Eun Kang's ghost. She did not . . . appear to me, not that night, or any other. I only ever . . . heard her. *A Gwisin's voice is typically high-pitched or deep*, yet this voice was somewhere in between.

Her voice was all I had to go by, though sometimes she spat her words right into my ear; when I put my finger in my eardrum, I could feel her spittle on my fingertip, sticky as snail-slime.

And once, I swear I felt her lank hair brush across my face. Korean ghosts are commonly known to do this.

I understand your look of skepticism. Despite my susceptible nature, I was doubtful throughout the experience.

The dead don't speak, I said to myself one time after a brief visit. I said it in my mind, so quietly I could scarcely hear the thought.

The dead can speak, she responded. *But you don't want to hear what we have to say, so you sew our lips together with clear thread, and you wire our jaws shut.*

And there was a . . . level, not only of information but of emotion in some of the things she uttered that I don't think I could muster:

Yes, I did hear a noise outside, she whispered to me, *but I took it for a possum or a raccoon, the rustle of an animal. When he came in, I said, "Hello, can I help you?" But let's get to the good part, that's what you're dying to know, aren't you? So you want to know what it was like? To die, like that? Well, when I looked into my killer's face, which was too close, I saw God's face, which was too far away. Though I could smell God's breath, which was even more putrid than my killer's. I called out to God to intercede, to mediate the dispute, but when the Almighty Fool did not respond, when I heard my own voice reflected back at me, echoing in the emptiness, merging with the voice of my killer—near the end I could not tell our voices apart—I saw God for what he was, or is or is not: not so much an absence, as an abscess, a festering Void, a gaping Hole from which creation pours forth. I saw that all of creation gets sucked back into that Hole. I looked up, past my killer's innocent face—near the end I could not tell God and my killer apart—and saw I was being welcomed into the arms of an immense and merciful (or do I mean merciless?) Hole . . .*

    I hope you're getting all this, she said to me and laughed. *You should call this one "My Murder Was the Irrefutable Proof of God."*

Tim had been gone for most of this period but came back for a bit. He started sleeping in the bed in his office. He initially put it down to jetlag but eventually came out with it: "I can hardly bear to be around you. You're acting really off, like you're . . . far away. Whenever I get up in the night to take a leak, I see the light under your door. What are you doing? Look at those circles under your eyes. Are you getting any sleep?"

    He was not mistaken; this . . . experience was having an impact on my sleep pattern that could not be considered positive.

    "I think you need to talk to someone," he said before he left for another month-long residency.

    Didn't he know that was the problem, that I was already talking too much, to someone, something?

There was a good week when I was utterly convinced this truly was Eun Kang. She must be biding her time to show herself to her killer, I thought; she's waiting for the right moment to creep or seep into his cell, so she can hang him with the sturdy pink umbilical cords of her two boys.

It seemed equally conceivable I was the reason Eun Kang was lingering. She was putting pressure on me, until I got her story right, until the pressure was so extreme I would need to tell someone her story. The killer was of no interest to her; I was the one she was intent on haunting.

Toward the end of our . . . acquaintance, things went a little funny. I've heard that happens with Gwisin. They turn.

She would come but she wouldn't say anything. I would sit there in bed for hours, waiting for her to speak, listening to her raspy breathing.

I suspected that I was now the object of Eun Kang's wrath and she was beginning to . . . resent me for knowing too much. Or too little: *If the Gwisin sends a message and the human fails to understand, the ghost may become somewhat aggressive.*

Then, out of nowhere, she would spit out her sentiments at an alarming rate:

Death makes fiction of us all, she drooled in my ear.

The dead don't give a shit about your eulogies or your elegies.

The fourth Fate is the worst Fate.

As far as I'm aware, Korean ghosts and ghosts in general ultimately leave, though some are reluctant to depart, even when they've had their revenge and their work is done.

Eung Kang left abruptly, but before she did she came to tell me this:

I'm bored with you, she said. *And the world. I see it for the dull place it is. I'm heading off to the Underworld, so I can surf on its hearse-black sea. Besides, it's a much safer place to raise two children.*

And to answer yet another of your inane questions, of course I didn't know. I didn't wake up that Thursday morning with a bad feeling in my bones and then brush the feeling away. When I went to surf that afternoon, I had no idea that time in the ocean, its briny graceful waste, would be my last.

You think that's why I was so crazy about the beach that summer? I'm not a fucking seer. I just wanted to catch some waves. But hey, didn't I see you there? I was coming out of the ocean as you were heading in. Or was I heading in as you were coming out? I forget, but I remember seeing you and smiling, I recognized you from the deli, your unwelcoming face, like a house that's been boarded up, but you didn't recognize me. I must have been coming out of the water because you looked right at me, then, as if I were transparent, already a ghost, you looked right through me to the sea and its briny elemental grace.

That was a couple of months ago. I'm still, as they say, . . . processing the events. I don't know if Eun Kang finished her task, attained a sense of completion. I don't think she could decide if she needed me to shred her story, until it was unrecognizable, or perfect it, but she kept her promise. I haven't heard from her since. I can't say I'm not relieved. I've thought about going back to her house, but I don't dare to, unless you want to come with me.

To restate my question from earlier, *who was she?* My doubts have returned. All along, I was just telling myself a story, right? The entire episode was an understandable side effect of watching one too many Asian horror movies, of reading and thinking too intently about such a morbid subject.

I filled that notebook. I transcribed *her words* so hastily, I could barely read my own handwriting. I no longer keep it on the bedside table. That seemed the sensible thing to do.

Eun Kang ceased talking to me, but that feeling I was telling you about, the heavy gray feeling that diffused into my heart one Thursday night in December, it's still there. I never found out if it's analogous to the feeling that transpired in Eun Kang's heart—I meant to ask. It seems to have developed tiny hooks. I can feel its hooks as I'm talking to you. So I guess I'm still haunted, even if it's a haunting of a linguistic nature.

Death Dream #1

The last time I got talking to God, we really got into it. You're right: if we're being logical, I was talking to myself. Anyway, I asked him if he had already planned when I was going to die and how I was going to die, if my death was written down somewhere, inscribed in advance. He said yes and then he coughed and went into specifics. The connection was staticky; I could make out a word here and there, but the most crucial details were inaudible.

Have you ever dreamt of your own death? I've had a number of dreams where I'm about to die in all manner of violent ways, and I wake up just before the final moment, but one time I dreamt I was really dead.

Actually it was more involved than that; I think I was alive *and* dead. I was walking down the hallway of a seedy hotel when I came to a little room. Inside the room there was nothing but a floral mattress, covered in stains, and lying on that mattress, coiled around one another, were three or four versions of myself. These . . . variants looked just like me, except they were even paler and skinnier, and there was something sensual and snakelike about their movements. I couldn't see their eyes because they were all wearing black wraparound sunglasses, the style I've been wearing since I was a teenager. With the conviction that comes in dreams, and that I lack in waking life, I knew I had died and shedded myself, and I stood there in the doorway and studied my dead snaky selves.

The dream was brief and for the most part uneventful, but allow me to interpret it in light of how it both meets and challenges our assumptions about death:

170

Although death will surely involve a total and absolute demolition of space, a flattening, this dream preserves our expectation that death will be spatial, three-dimensional, even if it is a small, squalid room in a flea-bag hotel.

More surprisingly, death may result not in the end of the self, its erasure or eradication, but the compounding of the self, its multiplication.

Given the dream's erotic atmosphere, and the knotted bodies of my snaky selves, this appears to support the inextricable link between sex and death. But those selves of mine only appear to be screwing. There is no genital contact, no sex is taking place. We postulate that sex and death are tangled together, but it's possible that sex is of no consequence. Death *is* sex. We're all virgins, pale versions of ourselves, until we penetrate or have been penetrated by death.

That's why I don't go inside the room. This is the most important aspect of the dream. I want to go in, but I know that if I do, if I go in and untangle the knot, unravel the secret of death, the secret of myself, I will have to join them. So I must not cross over the threshold. Death will destroy all our assumptions. Until then, death must remain impenetrable.

Data

*One day, two strangers will wander around a cemetery and
chance upon our graves. They'll glance down at our names
and the dates, gloss over the slightness of our epitaphs.
They'll keep wandering, looking absently at all the headstones. They'll think quietly, with such certainty: this will
never happen to us.*

Whenever I'm at Holy Cross, I get overwhelmed by thoughts, and
one thought overwhelms all the others: I'm being deceived. Sure, I
know that there must be actual people buried in the ground, people
whose lives were composed of radically varying percentages of joy and
disappointment, anonymity and fame; there must be corpses and skeletons concealed behind the names, but I don't quite . . . believe it. I find
it difficult to suspend my disbelief, just like I have trouble doing that
when I go see a play at the theater.

It's not like I haven't tried to shift this perception. I've stood and
crouched by so many gravesides, to see if I could . . . pick up on anything. I even put my ear to the grave of Sharon Tate, like that last photo
of her, taken the morning of her death, where her hairdresser, who
would also die that night, has his ear to her swollen belly.

I mean, it's not that I expected to have some vision like Bernadette,
to witness the voluptuous blonde apparition of Tate in her blood-
spattered paisley bikini, breast-feeding her eternally hungry baby, but
you would think, given the intensity of what happened to her, there
might be some residue, some trace.

But all I got was dirt on the knees of my trousers and I didn't sense anything. Same goes for the rest of the cemetery. The grounds feel sort of blank, sterile, as if every square yard has been disinfected, stripped of all distinguishing characteristics and shorn of all memory. Maybe death's just more laid back on the West Coast. Or you need a special machine to tap into the energy of the dead, like those metal detectors people use at the beach. I should see if anyone makes such a machine, because I've never picked up on the slightest vibration. I can't shake the feeling we're being fooled and there's nothing in any of the graves; the plots are all empty, like joke gift boxes with nothing inside.

I think it might have been easier for people in the old days, when death was more visible, on display, when they beheaded men in public then placed their heads on spikes.

Perhaps I should have become a grave robber, like in the books I read as a kid. I had great respect for these men who worked only at night, who were searching for rings and watches and jewels and gold— unless they were connected to scientific exploits, I don't believe the skeleton was the primary goal. My esteem for this occupation was so strong, one day at school when the teacher asked me what I wanted to be when I grew up, I said in all seriousness: *I want to be a grave robber.*

My ambitions have changed; even if you offered to help me and we dug up one grave, and the next and so on, until we had exhumed everyone, until our hands were scraped down to the bone and our fingernails broken, it wouldn't get us anywhere. The names on the headstones don't directly correspond to the bodies that have been so neatly packed away. Like all cemeteries, Holy Cross is a haphazard collection of raw data, printed matter, information to be mourned, information that may be used in a report to provide evidence, but of what? Not that these remains were once human. That's way too open to interpretation. How would you begin to prove that?

My Grandfather's Hemorrhage

If you listen carefully, you can hear the guy who inscribes the headstones — what do you call that guy? A mason? A tomb engraver? — sharpening his chisel and preparing the stone that will mark your grave. Such work must require a steady hand. If you keep listening, you might even hear him tapping away, chiseling your name slowly, so he doesn't have to hurry, to make sure your headstone is ready on time and the letters are shaped beautifully and your name is spelled correctly.

I come from a long line of ghosts.

By the time I was born, my mother's father had been dead ten years. Ten years, in the grave. Is it safe to say I did not know him?

In photos, with his white hair, in his elegant three-piece suits, the chain of his fob watch suspended between the lower button of his waistcoat and its left pocket, William Wildy looked like a ghost, or a funeral director: someone from another era. After all, he was born in the nineteenth century, 1892 or thereabouts.

Curious about this dignified man whom I was allegedly descended from, I would tug at the hem of my mother's skirt and ask her questions.

She wouldn't say much. He drove an old-fashioned car, *a real tin lizzie*. He invariably wore a suit, even when he wasn't working. He was the head of customs, oversaw all of Australia's imports and exports.

"I took you to see him once, his grave at Fremantle cemetery," she would tell me. "You were young, so you probably don't remember."

"Yes, I do," I would tell her. "We left some flowers. You showed me his name on the headstone; that's how I learned to read."

"That's right," she would say. "Now you run off, I've got things to do."

W-i-l-l-i-a-m. W-i-l-d-y.

This was everything I knew about my granddad. A name, an anecdote, a few facts. But not so long ago, my mom talked about her father on the phone. I forget how he came up. She told me about the last time she saw him.

That was in 1960. My mother had left Australia to marry her Scottish husband. They lived in Scotland for a while, in Motherwell, with my gran, then moved to London. My grandfather and his wife, Hilda, hadn't seen their daughter for a few years; they had never met her husband or their two grandchildren, Rory and Fiona. They wanted to check up on her.

So they traveled by ship from Australia to England. At the time, the voyage from the port of Fremantle to Portsmouth, where the ship docked, took six weeks.

By the way, did I mention I haven't seen my mother in thirteen years? None of my family. I can't quite explain why I haven't made the trip home. But I can tell you that during this period, my mother's voice has taken on its own identity.

William and Hilda Wildy arrived early in the morning, when it was still dark.

They took a train to the tiny basement flat—*small as a postage stamp*—that my mom and dad rented in Cricklewood in North West London.

Initially, my father was shy around his in-laws. This shyness never fully dissolved.

"But it was a wonderful reunion," Mom said, "everyone so excited to see everybody, even with the cold and the cramped conditions."

They did a lot of catching up, a lot of cooing over the babies, discussing who resembled whom. There was a fine layer of salt on my grandparents' belongings, their suitcases and my grandma's hat box. Rory (or was it Fiona?) started licking the salt off my granddad's face as he held his grandchild in his arms.

When my mother asked her parents how the voyage was, they said *it was fine. The food was tolerable.* Her dad told her they had seen a burial at sea.

"It was an impressive sight," he said. "As the coffin slipped from its black canvas bag, it made quite a splash."

It was slightly disconcerting to hear my mother enunciate the words of her father, as if his voice were haunting her voice, like a so-called *voice from the grave.* I could almost, but not quite, hear his formal manner of speaking, his diction, his intonations.

My grandparents intended to stay for six weeks: six weeks to get there, six weeks in London, six weeks to get back.

"Your granddad liked order," my mom said. "And symmetry. He liked numbers to match up and things to be in their place. It was a habit he picked up from his work."

They did a spot of sightseeing, Buckingham Palace, Westminster Abbey. They went to the Tower of London and saw the jewels in the Jewel House and the cell in the White Tower where Edward IV's long-haired boys were imprisoned before they disappeared, only to turn up two centuries later as an incomplete, inconclusive set of bones. After morning tea, they viewed the gibbet where countless men were hanged for treason until they were all but dead, as a preface to being disemboweled and drawn and quartered, and paused briefly at the exact place where Anne Boleyn's head left her body for good.

But my grandfather's constitution was delicate, and a week into the trip, he had a brain hemorrhage.

My mother is into her crossword puzzles; she does one every morning without fail and is knowledgeable about the root meaning of words.

"That's when a blood vessel bursts and floods the brain," she explained. "*Hemorrhage* comes from the Greek and means *blood bursting forth*. But it can also mean a damaging loss of something valuable."

Near death, Granddad had to be rushed to the hospital.

His wife and my mother and the little ones visited him every day. Luckily the hospital was nearby and they could walk through the park and admire the roses.

What you could see of them. Mom told me that although London had outlawed coal burning—after the great smog of the 1950s that killed thousands of people in a matter of days—citizens were flouting the law and burning coal, despite a potential fine of hundreds of pounds. Just as they had disobeyed the law back in the thirteenth century, when King Edward I decreed that anyone caught burning coal would be put to death.

"If torture and death wasn't enough to deter someone," she said with a laugh, "why would a measly fine work?"

Consequently, the air was grimy. The petals of the roses were gray and blackened, *but if you put your face close enough, you could breathe in the perfume of the rose.* Whenever they got home, the white wicker of the prams and the babies' clothes were filthy.

I can almost hear the sound of my mother's voice telling me all this as I tell you: her diction, her manner of speech, her formal intonations. Like her voice is haunting my voice. Can you hear it too?

My grandfather nearly died. He recovered, but he was not himself. When he was conscious and able to speak, my mother inquired as to how he felt.

"Do you want to know how it feels to have a brain hemorrhage?" he told her from his hospital bed. "It's as if there is an avalanche in your brain and that avalanche buries all your memories and thoughts. Or the avalanche is comprised of your thoughts and memories and they bury one another until there's nothing."

"He certainly had a way with words," my mom said. "I think I picked that up from him. That must be where you get your leanings."

I come from a long line of ghosts who are interested in words.

My grandfather was never himself again. He kept on talking about their outing to the Tower of London. He was an excessively rational man, but he now claimed to have beheld the ghost of Anne Boleyn, carrying her own head; "I could discern the thin red line where her neck was severed," he said.

My mother was ready to tolerate one ghost sighting, but her father also maintained he had clapped eyes on the ghosts of the two dead blond Princes in the Tower, Edward and Richard. Mom decided to play along and asked him if he was scared.

"Not at all," he said. "I just wanted to cut their hair."

By the time he was well enough to be discharged from the hospital, over four weeks had passed. It was near the end of the trip. My mom attempted to persuade her father that they should change their tickets and extend their stay until he was strong enough to travel. But that would have meant losing their return tickets and having to pay for a new one-way, ten pounds each, a total of twenty pounds. *What a waste that would be.* My granddad had spent his whole life tallying numbers, determining tariffs. He was simply not prepared to do this.

Before my mother knew it, it was time to put her parents back on the ship and to say good-bye. Dad borrowed a car from a mate and they all drove down to the docks, early in the morning.

My grandparents stood on the deck, waving damp handkerchiefs.

"I can still see them up there," my mom said, "even though it was so dark, all I could make out were their silhouettes."

When my grandparents arrived home, they called their daughter. My mother asked about the passage, and her father referred to the burial from their first voyage, *the splash it made,* as if the two voyages had blurred into one.

"He sounded very frail," my mom said, "kept mumbling about bad omens, and his voice was just a wisp of what it used to be.

"This might sound peculiar," she told me, "but by then it was not so much his voice as the ghost of his voice."

Granddad did say he had read an Agatha Christie novel, a murder mystery set on an ocean liner, which he enjoyed. The rest of my grandfather's thoughts were lost at sea.

Two months after they returned, William Wildy died, not at sea but in his bed. It was a new bed he had recently purchased, *as if he had specifically gone shopping for a deathbed.*

My mother was unable to attend his funeral. The corpse would not wait that long. Her father would spoil. But when he died, she felt it.

"You know how they say you can sense when someone dies, someone very dear to you?" my mom said, a quaver in her voice. "I was home by myself, well the kiddies were there, and I had just put them down for their naps. So I made myself a cup of tea and began doing a crossword puzzle. I don't remember the first clue, but it had seven letters, I remember that. And as I tried to figure the word out, I got the most uncanny feeling, I can't quite describe it, like something . . . well, like something floating through the air and into me and for no reason I burst out crying. What a ninny, I thought, crying over a crossword puzzle! Wouldn't you know, my mother calls a half hour later, telling me Dad had died. Isn't that remarkable, how I could sense this, across the ocean, thousands and thousands of miles away?"

W-i-l-l-i-a-m.

After receiving this news, my mother stared at the black telephone in their landlady's hallway; it had always struck her as a miraculous technology, but suddenly it looked ominous, black as a hearse. She realized she would never get to speak to her father again. Her father's voice had . . . fled the earth.

Distraught, she sat down and went back to her crossword puzzle; its blank white boxes demarcated by fine black lines had also taken on a menacing value. She completed it, except for that one word.

W-i-l-d-y. Pronounced not *wild-e*, but *will-d, d* like the letter, *will* like the legal document in which a person expresses how their possessions are to be disposed of and distributed after their death, when they have no need for possessions because they are . . . indisposed.

The one object William Wildy took with him, one he thought might come in handy, was his fob watch, hidden in the waistcoat of the black three-piece suit he was buried in, a suit he had made to measure on Saville Row in his last week in London. In his will he insisted the watch be wound by the mortician right before the coffin lid was closed.

And in all these years," Mom told me, "I've only dreamt of him once. I didn't know it was Dad at first. He was in the kitchen, dressed rather casually, a shirt with the sleeves rolled up and some pants a laborer might wear, spattered with paint. He wasn't dressed like himself or behaving at all like he did when he was alive. He was being very untidy, opening cupboard doors and not closing them, spilling milk and jam on the floor, and cursing!

"Even so, you would think I would have been pleased to see him, but I was petrified. A bit like Mary and Martha when Jesus raises Lazarus. It was a good reminder that resurrection is nice to think about but would be terrifying if you were faced with it. In truth, the only thing more disturbing than someone you love dying is the same individual coming back from the dead."

When my mother came to the end of her story, which, I suspected, she was telling for the first and only time, I reminded her of the day she took me to the cemetery to visit Granddad's grave and taught me to read her father's name etched into the stone.

Mom was silent and then laughed.

"I've never told you this, dear," she said, "but we never went to his grave. I did take you to the cemetery, but I couldn't find his plot. I looked for a while, but it was so hot and my shoes were pinching my feet, so I gave up and left the flowers on someone else's tombstone. I'm not sure how you got that idea into your head; I'm sorry, I shouldn't have humored you, I think you just learned to read the usual way."

She laughed again, I laughed as well, and beneath our laughter, within it, there was a puzzle, a clue, a question.

Yes, I think it's safe to say I did not know my grandfather. The fob watch must have stopped keeping time long before I was born. Yet from my mother's story and our mutual fabrications, I feel I have a better sense of him than many people I know who are supposedly living.

Like my granddad, I'm a rational man. I like order, symmetry. From where I stand, here in this other cemetery, Life and Death can be viewed as a system of imports and exports. I picture William Wildy in the afterlife, head of customs, supervising the incoming and outgoing flow of goods, ensuring the duties are collected and there are no discrepancies, no entry of items into the realm of Life or Death that are *restricted or forbidden.*

Now I remember how the subject of Granddad came up. My mom was wondering if I was planning a trip home. Before she got off the phone, she asked again.

"Any thoughts on when you might visit?"

I gave her my usual line: work was busy, it was hard to get time off, they were so inflexible, I would put in another request, I'm sure they would agree soon . . .

"Well," my mom said, "that will give me something to look forward to."

I watched her voice waft out of the receiver, a separate entity, a disembodied spirit. My mother is frail and getting on in years; a feeling floated in the air, in the thousands of miles between us, a sadness I cannot talk about: not with her, not with you, not with anyone.

I come from a long line of ghosts intent on self-deception.

I still can't believe he made the trip," Mom said, drifting back to talk of her father. "It went so quick. It was like your grandparents disembarked and I saw them for a second and then they got back on the ship. But I'm so glad I had the chance to see him that one last time, and he had the chance to see me."

Immortality

The only law I'm interested in breaking is the law of death,
but there is no way to defy this law. There is no way to keep
death from you and me and the handful of people I'm actually
close to, too close to, closer than is humanly possible.

I like that idiom, *at death's door.* I don't know where the turn of phrase comes from, and I don't think it's meant to inspire hope, but I like its intimations: if there is a door between life and death, even if the door is open, it is conceivable we can shut the door, ignore anyone who knocks at the door; we can lock the door and lose the key.

In *The World Book Encyclopedia,* between "Death Adder" and "Death Cup," there is a short entry on the legal term "Civil Death," or "Death, Civil." As I remember it, when someone *has not been heard from for a period of time,* say, seven years, *although this individual might still be alive, he can reasonably be assumed to be dead.* The guy's wife can remarry her chauffeur or her gardener; his heirs can divide up his things. But if that person turns up, *the law will make every attempt to restore what is his, as far as this is possible.*

I was unable to fit *civil death* into my book report, but this designation continues to intrigue me.

If you can undergo *a civil death,* perhaps you can elude *natural death* and all its accoutrements—unconsciousness, decomposition, nonbeing, the void, etcetera. Isn't there a loophole in every contract, even the contract of existence? If you can disappear from the law's circumscription, perhaps you can also . . . disappear from God's field of vision, until he can no longer see you with his bloodshot all-seeing eye, and, after a period of time, say, seven years, he will reasonably assume that you are dead and order the Destroyer to just . . . forget about you.

I need to find another individual who will really stand in for me. Would you want to do it? I'm looking for someone truly selfless who will serve as my stunt double, my body double during the tedious, dangerous business of dying, so while the scene is darkening I can be off . . . somewhere else.

If there were an actual hole we went through when we died, it would make things so much simpler. Imagine if we could pin down its location, in a region that's remote but can still be identified on a map. Then we could go there, just like Charles Manson took his Family to Death Valley, to look for this hole that he believed led to the other side, a black land *where the rivers run upside down.* When he sent out his followers to search for the hole in their black '58 Chevy, he made them wear these black capes, which looked like cheap Halloween costumes moms would rustle up for their kids at the last minute.

Manson thought they had found it when they came across Devil's Hole, a geological formation east of the Funeral Mountains; this geothermal pool leads to all these underground caves that are hundreds of thousands of years old. He sent some of his Family down into the hole, but the water was too hot and too deep: apparently Devil's Hole is bottomless, more or less, no one knows exactly how deep it is, divers have gone in there and never come out, their skeletons are still diving.

Maybe you and I should go on a quest for this hole. I've always wanted an excuse to go to Death Valley, which is listed in *The Encyclopedia* after "Death Penalty" and "Death Rate": a treacherous region that is not a valley at all, but a very long, very wide ditch called a *graben; a popular winter resort area* that used to be full of mining towns, where *today only cluttered debris remains.*

Manson failed, but perhaps we won't. My goal is relatively easy. He thought paradise, or his warped goth-hippieish version of it, was waiting for him and his friends on the other side, but paradise does not entice me. If I found the hole that leads to the afterlife, right after I took a peek to see what's going on inside, I would cover it with some of that debris, planks of wood or a piece of sheet metal that matches its circumference, no matter how narrow or how wide. The thing Manson and I do share is we both want to keep some people safe. With your assistance I would board up that hole, nail it shut.

Is there a false panel between the world and the afterlife, like the false bottom in the upright black box a magician employs in his vanishing act? With regard to our vanishing act, we have to locate or construct this false panel. We have to figure out how to trick decomposition. We haven't perfected the routine. We have to keep practicing.

At school we had to memorize those trippy lines from that more reputable self-styled prophet, the ones about *everyone dying yet living forever and never ever dying even if they die*. His words were confusing, like a tongue twister, and in my mouth they came out all wrong.

In my head the Resurrection remains unavoidable, irresistible yet vague. The Son of God comes back to life, floats through doors, then vanishes. Though I just remembered another part of the story I enjoyed, where Mary Magdalene goes to the tomb and it's empty and she cries and then she turns around and Jesus is there, but she thinks he's the gardener! Then she realizes he's not the gardener and goes to embrace Jesus, but he won't let her touch him. Mary Magdalene thinks he's acting kind of distant, but it's nothing personal; it has something to do with the conditions of the Resurrection.

Essentially, I'm still confused. The Resurrection complicates things, clouds our judgment. There is the possibility lurking in the back of my mind—faint as lead pencil—that when someone dies, they'll rise up from the dead. If I mistrust what I'm seeing, they will take my finger and insert it into their gaping side.

When the sun hits the side of the mausoleum at Holy Cross, the whiteness is blinding. It makes me want to graffiti its spotless surface. Something like, *Immortality doesn't exist, just ask Lazarus. He knows the void. He remembers the void, its contours. He knows he has to return to the void.* Or something more straightforward such as *Immortality is necessary, it keeps the void at bay.*

I seem to recall another book from childhood. There was one story in that book I especially loved, and I would ask my mother to read it to me, to help me go to sleep. A story about a king who was granted a wish, I don't remember why. Anyway, the king wishes for eternal life, and he gets it.

At first he's elated, but pretty soon he finds immortality isn't all it's cracked up to be. Everyone around him, everyone the king loves, withers and dies, filling him with sorrow. Although immortal, his physical self ages; that's one of the sneaky clauses of the wish: he seeks out company, but he has become so gnarled and hideous, covered in sores, that no one can even look upon him.

I forget how the story ends. I'd fall asleep while my mother was reading. I think whoever gave the king his wish finally reverses it and he dies and it's a weirdly happy ending. Or he endeavors to kill himself, employing a variety of methods, but none of them work—that's the hitch to deathlessness—and the king just goes on and on and is unbearably lonely.

Do you know this story? Did your mother read it to you? Am I getting it wrong—was the wish a curse endowed by some witch? Regardless of the story's form or its outcome, let me speak candidly: I would welcome the opportunity to experiment with immortality, whatever the conditions or the cost or the loss or the penalty, whatever the side effects.

An Encounter

*"I want to cross the line between life and death," he said,
"back and forth, right to left, left to right, until the line fades
in front of your eyes. . . . I want to disintegrate the line between
life and death," he said, "until that line no longer exists."*

In all my visits to Holy Cross, I've only had one proper conversation. It
wasn't so long ago. I was sitting on a bench when this guy came over
and sat down next to me. He was small and pale with dark spiky hair,
and he was clutching a skateboard. I had noticed him earlier, in his
T-shirt and his black jeans, leaning up against the cemetery gates.

We got to talking, and, as it turns out, we had some shared interests.
I was meant to head back to work, but the guy wanted to hang out. So I
called in sick. I know it was foolish—my coworkers and students could
see me from the university's north-facing windows—but I don't think
they're that observant, and anyway, as soon as I enter the gates, it's like
I become unseeable. I live such an orderly life; I needed some disruption.

The guy, who told me his name, but I didn't catch it, pulled out a
joint. He tucked his skateboard under his arm and we went behind the
grotto to smoke. He had this lighter decorated with little skulls, each of
the skulls wearing a crown. As we smoked, I told him how much I liked
it. *Here, you can have it*, he said.

We began to walk, and as we wandered, we talked. For once, the
weed, which was damn strong, had the opposite effect and loosened my
tongue.

*Although Holy Cross is, geographically speaking, a small pocket situated
inside Culver City*, I told him, hoping to impress my young friend by

speaking in the voice I use when I lecture, *I suspect the geographical relationship between Life and Death is the exact opposite: Life is a small pocket situated inside of Death, which is much larger than Life, and surrounds it, just like West Berlin was surrounded by the former East Germany, making it an enclave—one of the few terms I remember from geography—to that country, a territory whose geographical boundaries lie completely within another territory, to which it has no political connection. Similarly, Life is an enclave to Death, completely enclosed within Death's alien domain, whose inhabitants are of a distinct and separate culture and nationality.*

Or, I said, my voice acquiring a calm yet manic confidence, a rhetorical assuredness I had never experienced when broaching the subject of death, *to borrow the only term I remember from math, specifically geometry, a discipline that seems more apt, the spatial relationship between Life and Death is one of inscription: Life, which is an abstract shape, is inscribed inside Death, a different abstract shape; their boundaries touch but never intersect. This would mean that Life isn't as small,* I said, wondering if I was even using the mathematical concept correctly. *Life fits as snug inside Death as a corpse in its cozy coffin, but Death remains a closed self-governing system, under its own jurisdiction, outside any municipality.*

These were just some of my "insights," which probably make no sense now. But I was on a roll, and as the guy produced another joint, I began to tell him other things, things I hadn't told anyone. Not even you. It wasn't only the weed; he felt so familiar, like I had known him for a thousand years. He reminded me of someone, though I couldn't put my finger on who; he reminded me of a bunch of people, crudely stitched together.

It was more an air about him than what he said; in fact, now that I think of it, he said so little, it was like he said nothing at all. He mainly listened while I rambled, giddy in his presence. Though the few things he did say really resonated with me.

We walked everywhere that day; I went to sections I had never been, in the far reaches of the cemetery, Holy Cross's extremities: section CC, for the Holy Martyrs, where all the nuns are buried in their veils and the priests in their heavy black robes; and section BB, which has the tiniest headstones I've ever seen. With their lacy borders, they look like decorative pillows, bearing nameless epitaphs like *Before you were born, I knew you* and *Now you are reborn*, statements skirting the issue in the area for the Holy Innocents, for all the unrealized, unbaptized souls who won't even end up in Limbo, though didn't the Vatican cancel that intermediary space in the 1980s?

Then we found ourselves in that isolated area on the cemetery's eastern edge, where there are literally no bodies, section DD, the Shrine to the Unborn, for those beings whose lives are annulled inside the womb. As we rested on the memorial bench with flames carved into its black marble, an image that wasn't exactly comforting, I had what can only be called a revelation, as if my mind were also heading to its outer reaches: *They say that first wail of newborns is due to the first painful intake of breath into our tiny lungs, which are like toy accordions,* I said, as my friend pulled out a Swiss Army knife and began to carve into the marble. *But perhaps, as soon as we exit the mother, in our infantile wisdom we sense what is happening, we know what we are in for, there is no being born without dying, we're already dying before we're even born, we feel it in our weirdly soft bones. Maybe we even know how we're going to die. If we could, we would claw our way back into the womb, using our fingernails, delicate as mother of pearl. As soon as we were safely inside, we would grab that umbilical cord and hang ourselves from the womb's pink gallows. But humans in green gowns and green masks are threatening us with their shiny surgical instruments—we've been forced into existence, at knifepoint—and the couple who tricked us, coerced us into actuality, are holding onto us way too tight, screaming at us in a foreign language. Bloody and inarticulate, we can't communicate any of this, so we make our first wail, which can be roughly translated as "I've been fooled, I'm fucked, the only way out of this mess would have been not to be born at all!"* I said to my friend who was still scratching away at the marble as my thoughts ignited in his presence.

The unborn were starting to weigh on me, the idea of un-being is remarkably heavy, so we trudged up the hill to the mausoleum, to the chapel, where we dipped our hands in the font with the holy water and made the sign of the cross, first on ourselves, then on each other—he even took a sip of the water straight from the font, like a dog drinking from a dog-bowl, he was just fooling around, but I found the gesture to be sacrilegious and *fonts are a well-known source of bacterial infection*— and we helped ourselves to an open box in a hallway, full of the crucifixes that are *complimentary with every funeral package.* Then we smoked yet another joint in the maintenance yard behind the mausoleum, where we saw an amazing thing: coffins stacked on top of one another; so many that if you kept on stacking them, eventually you would scrape the underside of the moon. The coffins appeared to be made of pale wood, but we went up to touch them and they were cardboard. They must have been for cremation, which requires a container that is highly combustible. You know how I am with weed; I started to ponder the notion of *a cardboard corpse,* which amused the guy to no end; we kissed behind those makeshift caskets and his mouth tasted sour and his breath smelled of burning leaves and in the tangle of our tongues I lost my *complimentary crucifix* and my sense of time and the day kind of shredded away.

It was getting late, time for the cemetery to close, to lock the gates, which they do with a big padlock like an oversized chastity belt. Needless to say, this only serves as a deterrent to the living, who could never slip between the gate's bars, while the dead can just flutter through them. *Do you want to stay here overnight?* the guy said. *I know another way out.* He took me by the hand and led me to the western edge of the cemetery, where we walked along this open drain that runs down the edge, ending in this sort of deep circular concrete void at the cemetery's boundary. I think it's what they call a *culvert. Look,* he said, *you can just slide under the fence here.* He even demonstrated how to slip out, then slipped back in and looked right at me with these seaweed-green eyes, his gaze filled to overflowing with a vacancy I was ready for. *So how about it?*

Sure, I said. Tim was working somewhere in the Midwest, and I thought our dog would survive the night. So we hid down there in that concrete void, listened to the traffic going by on Mesmer, waited for the cemetery employees to leave. As it was getting dark the streetlights switched on, illuminating the tattoos on this stranger's arms, a series of skulls heaped one on top of the other, that boy was a walking Golgotha, skulls climbing up his arms like roses on a trellis; some of the skulls were smiling, some were serious, some had roses blooming in their empty sockets. His jeans looked somewhat greasy in the light, as if they hadn't been washed in weeks. Up close, I could see blond roots in his dark hair. My mind kind of . . . cleared and I told him, *You know, I really should get home and feed my dog. Sorry, can we take a rain-check? Can I get your number?* He kind of snapped. *Fuck you,* he said, and stared at me with this dark-green vacancy. As I scrambled under the metal fence, he leapt out of our little void, his skateboard still tucked under his arm. I stood up and watched from the other side of the fence as he ran off in the direction of the mausoleum, until he was just a silhouette.

The Ballad
of Sandra Golvin

There's a storm drain at the cemetery, not far from my bench. After it has rained, it sounds like the drain is singing, like the dead are singing. Can you hear it? Do the dead ever sing to you?

I heard she died of ocular cancer. I heard she said some very strange things. I heard she looked directly into the sun.

I heard her eye was bothering her; that's how it begins.

I met Sandra not long after I moved to LA, sometime between Mike and Robert. She lived in the Venice canals with four other women. The arrangement was . . . complicated. There was a Brazilian woman who was Sandra's ex and now had a new wife. I'm pretty sure one of the women in the other couple was the wife's ex. The two couples were in the main house, which had two stories and was painted bright yellow with green trim. Sandra occupied an adjacent unit on the same property: one story, painted dark crimson.

This was back when Tim was living by himself on North Venice Boulevard. On Sundays we used to walk his old dog Buddy in the canals. Sandra was often on her patio or in the front yard, so we would stop and say hey.

The first time I met her, I complimented the color of her house. "It's Blakean crimson," I told her.

"What the hell do you mean?" she said, her lips crinkling into a smile.

I explained the reference, the Blake poem about the sick rose, the invisible worm howling through the night, bent on destroying the lovers' bed of crimson joy.

"Where did you find this one?" she said to Tim, laughing. "Blakean crimson. I love it, that's wild," she said, staring at her house and forgiving the pretensions of a nervous young man. "That's wild."

In my memory, those walks in the canals were always a bit too sunny, but I can see Sandra through the glare. Her face was craggy and lined; she didn't wear makeup. She usually wore shorts and had these sturdy legs. Barefoot or in flip-flops, her toenails were gnarly, black with fungus. Sometimes they were painted with this brown, gooey homeopathic solution. Her voice was scratchy, like something was caught in it. Or a pubescent boy's voice on the verge of breaking.

If Sandra was inside and noticed us, she would come out, but she never invited us in. I only went inside her house once. I had started an MFA, to learn how to write, and a friend of mine from school, Sarah, who lived on an island off the coast of Washington, was looking for a sublet during one of our residencies. Sandra knew about this; Tim must have mentioned it. She was going out of town and offered to sublet her place. Sarah and I went over there to pick up the keys.

Sandra must have showed us around, but I can't visualize the layout or the furnishings. She gave Sarah a few instructions, most of which were regular, except for this business with the doors and the cats. Sandra had three cats; I forget their colors. I had caught flashes of them before, but they made themselves scarce during our visit. She was very clear that the sliding doors had to be kept open at night, so her cats could move freely.

"Are you sure that's safe?" Sarah asked. I think we were all standing about; we never sat down.

"Oh yeah," Sandra said. "It's hard to explain, I just . . . know that this place is protected."

Sarah, who is a reasonable human being, suggested that perhaps she could let the cats wake her up whenever they needed to go out; the thought of sleeping by herself in an unlocked house made her anxious. But Sandra was having none of it; she didn't want to mess with the cats' night patterns.

"I really don't want the cats to feel disoriented by your presence," Sandra said, eyeing Sarah. "I know this sounds weird but the cat thing is kind of a deal breaker."

Things got slightly tense for a moment, but Sarah said sure and they exchanged cash and keys. As we walked back to Tim's place and talked about how intense Sandra was, Sarah said no way was she going to sleep with the doors open; she would just let the cats paw at her and mewl to be let out.

Sandra had been so insistent, as if she felt the cats were guarding her home, defending the perimeters; if they were trapped inside it might tamper with the magic, leave her house open to evil spirits. She did have four cats, but one had just died and I remember her telling me one Sunday that she kept seeing the cat flickering past her, out of the corner of her eye.

Though she may just have been one of those crazy cat ladies, there was something witchy about Sandra. If she had been around in previous centuries, she would have been a target for people's suspicions. Neighbors would have gossiped: *I saw her shape-shifting into a feline form; I overheard her cats speaking grammatically perfect English, taught to them by their demonic mistress.* Those toenails of hers would have been seen as undeniable evidence, a weird witch marking.

Sandra looked even more witchy later. Her hair was short, brown with streaks of gray, but she grew it out, until it was long, so long that it curled down her spine in all these dappled shades of gray and silver.

The change in her hairstyle corresponded to a change in her life. Sandra had been a lawyer—I'm not certain what area of law she specialized in—but she began studying psychology. Eventually, she stopped her law practice, became a therapist and professor of psychology.

I've known many other Californians like her, who've undergone a similar midlife career change. They all had a crisis in meaning, I suppose, wanted to be doing something more authentic, more worthwhile, and psychology appeared to solve this dilemma.

I don't quite get it, these humans committed to working on themselves up until the grave. I don't believe I'll work out anything about myself until I'm in my grave, tucked in neat and tight.

However, I appreciated Sandra's passion for her subject, even envied it. One time as we chatted in her front yard, we got to talking about our classes. I had also graduated and was teaching at the same school as her, the one I'm still at today. She was teaching a class on psychological theory, and I asked if she was enjoying it.

"Oh God, yeah," she said, with her crinkly smile. "I love that stuff. With theory I'm like a pig in muck."

She asked about my class, which was on lit theory. I said it was fine, but my ambivalence must have come across. Sandra looked at me sternly. "You know, you should only do what you're passionate about."

The trouble is, then and now, I've never been that passionate about any form of work. I have to fake it.

I hope I don't have a midlife crisis and feel the urge to switch careers, to do something more meaningful, because I have no idea what that would be. I may have an obsession with you-know-what, but that fixation has nothing to do with passion.

Sandra was into dreams; that was the main thing, perhaps the only thing, we had in common. We both valued their obliqueness, their insoluble beauty.

One evening I was walking by myself in another section of the canals and I came across Sandra. The night was windy and her hair was tousled and straggly. She was wearing this big gray shawl that kept billowing behind her. I could tell something was . . . weighing on her, but I didn't want to ask if she was okay. In the abstruse branch of psychology in which she was immersed, it was taboo to ask this question.

As we walked together she began telling me about this dream she had had the night before. *In the dream, her mother was in a hospice in Florida and her cat Jackson was at the vet's in California and Sandra was having to fly back and forth to look after them. But her mom and her cat were sort of . . . shifting and blurring. Sometimes the cat was in the hospice, its weak, puny body in a huge bed, hooked up to the intricate breathing apparatus her mom had been connected to, and sometimes her mom was at the vet's, in a cage that was far too small for her. Tired of all the air travel, Sandra arranged to have a long IV tube join the mother in Florida to the cat in California, circulating blood and a mysterious healing solution. The infusion seemed to work: by the end of the dream, all three were in Sandra's apartment, and everyone was feeling better. Sandra was lying in bed, her mother beside her, the cat purring on her chest, all three sleeping peacefully.*

"Oh, has your mother been ill?" I asked.

"Yeah," Sandra said. "Actually, she died. I just got back from Florida."

I told Sandra how sorry I was, but she said not to worry.

"I doubt this will be as hard as the death of my cat a few years ago. Mothers are one thing, but I'm still torn up about Jackson. Smell that," she said, pointing to the canals, the mucky green-brown water, slimy with duck shit. "That's what the unconscious must smell like."

She turned to me and laughed. She had a gleam in her eye and a deranged look on her face, reminiscent not so much of a witch as a prophet from the Old Testament, one prone to rages and gnomic, enigmatic statements, recently returned from the desert.

I think that was the last time I talked to Sandra. Tim and I had moved in together, to another part of Venice, and his old dog had died—put to sleep with 80 ml of Nembutal—so we weren't walking as much in the canals. When we got our new dog, we walked her a different route. I might have seen Sandra once or twice in the elevator at work and said hello, but nothing more.

Basically, I . . . lost track of Sandra. Like I lose track of everyone.

And then Sandra died. Sandra had ocular cancer. Cancer of the eye. I didn't know there was such a thing. I guess there's a cancer for every section of the body, every subsection, every organ.

She went to the doctor one November because *her eye was bothering her*; that's how it begins. She received her diagnosis, was given nine months to live, and was dead by August, within nine months.

I must have really been out of the loop because I didn't know about any of this until after Sandra's death. I don't recall an e-mail from human resources. I was at work and saw a flyer for her memorial. The event was scheduled for a Saturday night, which made me reluctant to go but Tim said we needed to show up.

At the front of the room—A1000, a cavernous, nondescript space— a red and blue silk scroll hung above the stage, forming a backdrop. Apparently Sandra had this scroll over her bed: the bed she dreamt on, *the piece of furniture, typically a framework with a mattress and coverings*, that would become her deathbed.

On the scroll there was an image of a Tibetan deity. I don't remember her name; she had a third eye, but don't they all have third eyes? Bright red, she held a cleaver in one hand, a cup carved out of a human skull in the other hand, filled with blood. There were miniature skulls adorning this deity's forehead, and she was dancing against a background of thousands of eyes surrounded by flames. As she danced she was crushing some tiny guy beneath her left foot. By the look of things, she was a Dakini of the wrathful variety.

As people came up on stage and spoke of Sandra, their relationship to her, the microphone hissed; I didn't take much in. At memorials, when the living attempt to invoke the dead, I become very aware that language's primary function is to conceal, like the clouds of black ink that octopuses release to shield themselves from danger. The more we describe the dead, the less we can see them and the further away we get from them.

Though after the speeches, I heard and overheard some interesting notions.

Sandra's doctor, whom I used to be quite friendly with, told me that she didn't take any medication for a long time because she wanted to learn about death, and for that, she felt she needed to be lucid.

But when the pain became too much for her, she said, *Okay, give me the morphine.*

And from her morphine haze she began to speak in a shrill voice, like a little girl's. Her belly had swelled and she kept patting her stomach, like an expectant mother, asking the doctor when her baby was due.

"When people die," the doctor told me, "they say strange things. People habitually say strange things, but as they're dying, the things they say, and the way they say them, get even stranger."

I heard that Sandra thought she got the cancer from not wearing sunglasses. She was superstitious about dark glasses, hiding her eyes from people. She liked to sunbathe with her eyes open, staring straight into the sun.

A former student of mine and Sandra's told me that Sandra had called her and left a message on her voicemail, saying that she was dying and could she come over. Sandra was worried all her knowledge was going to die with her, and she wanted to pass that knowledge on. So the student visited Sandra once a week and sat by her bed with a tape recorder.

But she said Sandra couldn't articulate any of it; she couldn't put her ideas into words and it all came out scrambled, disconnected, incoherent, like Father Zossima's talk with Alyosha—that is, before Zossima gained some clarity and poured out his heart on the last day of his life in an unclouded and intelligible manner. Denied this clarity, in the end, Sandra asked her student to read to her; she just wanted to hear other people's voices.

I heard that Sandra spat and screamed at some friends who came to see her: *Get out! You think you're watching me dying, you think I'm here, but I'm not.*

I heard that Sandra's ex shaved her head and, per Sandra's instructions, saved her long gray locks and used them in a spell.

And I heard Sandra kept a journal, documenting those nine months, from the first day almost to the last, a chronicle of her . . . experience.

During the memorial—was it at the end or the beginning?—they played a song from my adolescence, by a band synonymous with the musical genre known as MOR, Middle of the Road. I understand this genre is popular for services, perhaps because it is so unlike the music bodies play on their deathbeds: they say it sounds like an entire brass band is marching inside of you to a gaseous, wheezing rhythm; as if every organ is part of an orchestra conducted by your soul, producing a screeching, rumbling racket that is not unlike feedback, the audio phenomenon that occurs when a fraction of the output of a machine is returned to the input of the same machine and retransmitted in a loop that is in some instances, like death itself, a self-corrective action.

I had never liked the song, but as I sat there and listened I became . . . overwhelmed with emotion. I believe this is the desired effect. It was a love song, and I thought of Sandra when she was young, the life she dreamt was ahead of her. I remembered Sandra's prickly kindness and it struck me that this was no longer the case because the dead are incapable of being kind. I had that tight, constricted sensation you get in your throat when you're about to cry, what they call *a lump in one's throat.*

When the song ended, someone came over to talk to Tim and me, and I didn't speak. I didn't talk until it was safe to do so; I waited until that tight sensation in my throat was gone.

In the weeks after, I had trouble sleeping. I would wake up in the night and think about Sandra. Clearly this was nothing new. How many hours have I spent in my life lying awake in the dark, directing my mind toward the departed, using this human capacity to form connected ideas about the dead?

After Sandra was presented with her diagnosis, after a man in a white coat handed down her death sentence, she must have had trouble sleeping too, trying to figure out . . . how to die.

What was it like, those nine months? Did every action and conversation take on a certain weight, a certain . . . significance? Or did the routine of dying become mundane, like everything else?

Early on, Sandra must have thought, *I feel normal, I don't feel any different, I'll be the exception.* But gradually, and then swiftly, her body must have acted so inexplicably she knew this was it.

One particular night, as my mind whirred, I tried to figure something out.

Just a month or two before I was riding my bike along the Grand Canal, on my way to the beach. I heard this . . . terrible noise coming from the direction of Sandra's house. At the time, I took it for one of her cats. It sounded like that god-awful yowl cats make when they're in heat, a vocalization that's not quite animal, not quite human, as if they're trying to speak, but their rough tongues end up deforming language, shredding it. Yet there was a quality to the sound that was not feline.

I did the math; this would have been late June or early July. The noise may have been Sandra prior to the morphine, shrieking as the pain was intensifying, as death was shredding her, deforming her into an organism not quite human, not quite animal.

Or was it Sandra and her cats, yowling, caterwauling along with her?

As I lay in bed, twisting and turning, I recalled Sandra's strict directives about the doors and the cats, her conviction that thanks to her pets, her home was secure. Sandra was right. Ocular cancer either originates in the eye and spreads outward to diverse locations in the body, far-flung regions, or stems from another internal organ and makes its way to the eye. There was no threat from anyone or anything outside. Her death came from within.

Unless Sarah, by locking the sliding doors, somehow broke the spell; the cats were unable to get out and the spirits clawed their way in, bringing death with them.

In the dark I was beginning to see that cats and the dead share specific characteristics: they are both nocturnal creatures; night is the time in which they are most active.

They both have superior night vision. Just as cats have those mirror-like layers at the back of their eyes, the dead's eyes must have some facet that allows their irises to dilate to such an extent they can let in all possible darkness and turn it into light.

But who inherited Sandra's cats? I wondered, tugging on the sheet that had coiled around my legs and pulling a blanket up to my neck. Perhaps they all died of grief; I've heard animals do that. Or did they burn the cats when they cremated Sandra, like they used to burn cats at the stake with their witch? Were the felines' ashes disseminated with Sandra's throughout the Santa Monica bay?

All my fidgeting woke up Tim, who retreated to his office. I grabbed my laptop, crawled back into bed, and looked up ocular cancer again, just to make sure I didn't have it.

On a site run by some eye institute, there was an illustration of an eye by itself: no face, no socket. There was another larger image of the eye from an interior perspective; it resembled a bloody red ball.

It seems if you catch eye cancer early enough and it's confined to the eye, you can do something about it, radiation therapy and a procedure called *enucleation*, which is the removal of the eye, but Sandra was beyond that.

I didn't appear to have any of the symptoms, but that's where it gets confusing, because the symptoms run from bulging eyes to a change in the color of your iris to poor vision to seeing flashing lights and shadows to a red painful eye to a tiny defect on the iris to no symptoms at all.

Still not sleepy, I searched for Sandra, for information on her. There was the usual disparate selection.

I skimmed the sites dealing with her professional achievements until I came to an article about her house in the *Los Angeles Times*. Sandra had been interviewed; she said when she went to inspect the property, her unit was gray, *a gray box*, but *as soon as she saw that gray box she knew she needed to live there*. She painted it crimson *to reveal the house's true character*.

I couldn't help but think that Sandra, given her propensity to the irrational, to all things magical, had viewed the premises not only as *a good investment* but as an augury; she had painted the walls a color to match the intensity of what awaited her. She had found a place suitable to die in, a house in which she could comfortably howl her way to death.

There was data available on an assortment of Sandra Golvins: names, like deaths, are not unique. Names are interchangeable, a dime a dozen. Sandra could have used this to her advantage: *No Death, it's not me you want, it's that other Sandra Golvin . . .*

I even tracked down a blog written by Sandra herself, but when I clicked on the link there was no text; the screen glowed white and I was informed *you have reached your viewing limit.*

Just as it was getting light, and the birds were stirring, I fell back to sleep.

At first I dreamt of what I had just been doing: staring at a screen. I was examining that eyeball from the medical illustration, but it looked more like one of the eyes from that Tibetan scroll. Instead of eyelashes, this eye had delicate flames fanning out from the rim. This eye was on fire. The flames began to singe and melt the transparent protective layer of the LCD monitor, the computer's own cornea and aqueous humor. I could smell the burning plastic, I could feel the heat, so I closed the laptop and fell asleep a second time, fell more deeply into the dream.

I found myself in a cave; it was pitch black. As my eyes adjusted, like the eyes of the dead are forced to adjust to the afterlife, I was able to identify three figures: Sandra with Robert and Mike. All three wore black rags and were long-haired, huddled over a cauldron like the witches from *Macbeth*; I was only in the cave a moment, but I knew these were my weird sisters, muttering something pertaining to my fate, prophesying at a volume so low I couldn't hear the words . . .

And then suddenly I was in Sandra's house, sitting up with her in bed. Medicines and potions cluttered the bedside table, along with a dog-eared copy of *As I Lay Dying*. On the cover was a German Expressionist painting of Sandra in her death throes.

Propped up by satin pillows, she was writing and drawing in that journal of hers, at a pace that was furious. She paused and showed me her work. Her handwriting was childlike: huge crooked letters, jagged and florid, a baroque scrawl. Her drawings were childlike and jagged as well: monsters with fangs and eyes stretched wide enough to take in death's horror, accommodate death's darkness.

Sandra was flicking the pages too quickly, and I couldn't read what she had written, so I tried to take the book from her, but that made her angry; she held onto the book tightly, clutched it to her breast, and then this black tarry stuff started to leak from her eye . . .

Sandra died three summers ago. Her place was sold last year. I don't know if her death was a determining factor, if the four other women were driven away by her raging, indignant ghost, or if it was simply a good time to sell. Surely the latter—real estate values in Venice continue to rise.

I've seen the guy who lives in her crimson box, lounging shirtless in a hammock in the front yard, drinking a beer, strumming a guitar. He sings softly, a song whose words only he can hear. Whenever I pass by, I want to ask him: *Do you ever sense her, do you ever catch her flickering past you out of the corner of your eye?*

To say that I was devastated by Sandra's death would be an overstatement. That itch in my throat at the memorial was just a Pavlovian, physiological reaction to that stupid song. I was much more upset when Tim's old dog died; when the vet applied the saline solution prior to the actual injection, I lost it. But Sandra's passing definitely . . . affected me, more than say Mike's or Robert's. Unlike their deaths, Sandra's somehow managed to . . . penetrate me.

Emotionally, I mean. Not metaphysically; there was nothing even faintly supernatural about it like that business with Eun Kang.

Though the frightful wailing that must have been Sandra—a distorted song, nothing middle of the road about it, erupting from her mouth like lava as she lay dying—was that a somatic expression of pure pain, or her calling out to me, reaching out? As she lay on her deathbed, did she really perform a kind of vanishing act; did her mind leave her body and fly around like a witch on her broomstick, *capable of flying anywhere, at any desired speed, at any height?*

And the dream where I was with her, where I was sitting so near I inhaled her death stench—that's the only dream I've ever had where my olfactory senses were working. When I recounted the dream to a mutual colleague Alma, at a faculty dinner where martinis were involved, she was impressed: "That wasn't just a dream, baby, that was Sandra trying to get back in touch with you; that was a vision."

I've since been unfaithful to Sandra; I've dreamt of others who have gone—as long as the dead are willing to inhabit my dreams, my sleep will always be troubled.

I wish I could train my unconscious and pay Sandra a return visit, so I could get another look at that book of hers, her death book, so I could . . . understand what it's like. Dying, I mean. Of all the books in the world, that's the one I most want to read. Would you like to read it with me? We could read it together. Someone must have inherited it; I should ask around. I would do just about anything to get my hands on that book.

Or maybe not. If I read what's in those pages, it would surely have a detrimental impact; I might never sleep again.

A Death Book

Every time I leave the cemetery, I feel I haven't learned much of anything. But as I walk between the rows of graves like rows of desks in a classroom, the dead are so quiet, they might be learning something. The dead know all these things we don't know. But they're so withholding. That's why I'm drawn to them. The dead know everything.

So I've been thinking of writing a death book of my own. This way, I could be done with it. Death, I mean. I could lay all these thoughts to rest.

I don't know though; it's a big undertaking. I'm not sure I'm up for it.

You could work on a book like that forever and never be satisfied, like one of those Gothic cathedrals that took centuries to build and destroyed generations of men in the process.

And if you ask me, I think this would be the wrong direction: instead of attempting to capture death's . . . vastness, a death book should be relatively modest in dimension, discrete as a grave in its proportions, yet full of hidden things, just as a grave offers the concealed promise of significance.

It could be as simple as the infinite death book I envisioned as a kid. The pages of this book were divided into three columns, like an old-fashioned library card, in this instance listing the date the individual was issued, the name of the individual who had borrowed their own identity, and their due date—as soon as the individual was returned, even if it was beyond their due date, a line was drawn through their name.

Simple or grand, the writer would keep coming up against the problem of . . . perspective. His viewpoint would be no more enlightening than the murderer who presents his book report; every murderer thinks he's undergone something awe-inspiring and shattering, he's been elevated to a higher plane, when all the time he was stuck in the anthropological world of observation, doing his best to make sense of a bundle of organs and emotions; it's the dead who experience everything, not intellectually, like the writer or the murderer, but viscerally, concretely. A death book written by the living, someone with no experience of decomposing? In a language that refuses to decompose?

Not only would writing this book be futile, given the idiomatic properties of death, it would also be dangerous. To describe the dead is to commit a violation, and the only thing worse is inscribing them, so their death becomes a permanent record. You would want the book to serve a protective, magical function, but it would more likely turn against you. Something as trivial as a comma placed incorrectly could send the Destroyer the wrong signal. And it wouldn't be good for the writer's health, getting so close to the dead.

I may not know much about death, but I know this: *we know nothing about death, absolutely nothing.* All those books that take on the subject are of no use to us. They're just trying to cover up death, like the slab of stone known as a ledger that covers a grave in its entirety. You would learn more from listening to a story told by a corpse whose tongue has shriveled in his head, and dried up like a flower, let's say a rose. Or from listening to the corpse's music; someone recently told me that a corpse is a kind of music box: the body cavities stretch open, and the skin unwraps itself, revealing the gift of the skeleton, over a soundtrack of popping, ripping, tearing noises. We might as well dig a huge hole in the desert, and bury every book written about death in this hole. A hole so deep we can't retrieve the books.

Even so, I'm tempted to try to write a book that moves, not the living, but the dead, who remain unmoved by our words, our music, our tears. I want to write it from a place where it's too dark to read or write. But I'm doing my best to resist the temptation.

The Hearses

*Look, they're about to lock the gates. But there's one last
thing I want to tell you. Why don't you come closer? Why
don't we have a race to see who can disintegrate first?*

Obviously I'm not at the cemetery. Obviously, I gave in. I didn't want
to—this book almost destroyed me, I came this close to destroying the
book—but I felt . . . compelled, as if someone really were whispering in
my ear, as if the dead were singing: *We'll let you write this book, but on
one condition, that you listen to us, that you let us in, that you let in the
disintegrations.*

I'm not sure where you are, but I'm at home, at my desk, applying
some finishing touches, touching the desk's wood for the thousandth
time, hoping I got the spell right and the book's rotten odor will throw
Death off my scent. I'm checking that the measurements are correct, so
this book's dimensions will match the circumference of the hole in the
world and seal the hole and protect you and me and the people I love.
I'm making sure the hidden clause is buried so deeply even God will
overlook it.

Far from the order of the cemetery, I'm surrounded by the disorder
of my office. All my files and death clippings are scattered about me.
That book I assembled on Eun Kang is around here somewhere . . .

Closer at hand is Aino's hourglass, the one she cradled in the palm
of her hand. I forgot to mention she noticed me admiring it and gave it
to me. *I won't need this where I'm going,* she said.

Okay, okay; she didn't exactly give it to me. She left that meeting
early and left the hourglass on the table. The meeting ended, and as the

room emptied, I lingered and picked up the tiny object, with the intention of giving it back to Aino the next time I saw her, but I don't think there was a next time and by then I had grown attached to her hourglass. I keep it on my desk, despite my grandma's warning about the dead coming back for their belongings; so far Aino hasn't and I've made good use of it.

I've been sitting here for years, playing with that hourglass as I write, turning it up and down in the palm of my hand. I don't feel like I've been writing so much as ingesting the dead, their lives ground down to a fine powder, like a cannibal engaged in a solemn ritual, striving to gain the dead's attributes and powers of immortality, but all I'm left with is a bitter taste in my mouth.

I feel dazed, as if I've been knocking my head against the desk, like *the brownish beetle that goes by the name of "deathwatch," which has the peculiar habit of knocking its head against wood, producing a ticking, rapping sound.* When heard in the dead of night, this causes superstitious people like you and me to believe *the sound foretells a death in the house, hence the insect's name.* That insect evokes real feeling in other humans; it gets its message across clearly and succinctly, without any ambiguity.

By comparison, my attempts at communication are inferior; every day, with death, language reaches its limit. It has taken me this long to see that it is not a question of translation: the dead are a distinct species from us. A species so alien we cannot talk to them or write about them just as we cannot breed with a corpse or a skeleton; we cannot exchange genes or ideas.

But the book is nearly done and lately, I've been flicking that lighter, a memento from my encounter with the guy at the cemetery; I keep it next to the hourglass. I'm flicking it right now. It's relaxing. The little crowned skulls are a reminder that death is sovereign.

When I got home that night, I had a strange sensation, as if a feeling dark yet light as a black ribbon had fluttered through the gates, followed me home, and pinned itself to my chest. I ignored the feeling until I fell asleep and dreamt, not of the young man from the cemetery but the boy from UCLA. Inside the dream nothing happened—he didn't say anything, he just stared at me—but I woke up to an awareness that something unspeakable had happened to him, as well as an awareness of something sticky on my belly. My first wet dream since I was a teenager. There was no connection between the content of the dream and my nocturnal emission; it had more to do with the dream's intensity, an intensity that needed a way out . . .

Wide awake, I went to my office and looked up the UCLA case. It had been awhile since I'd last checked, and there had been some new information. The boy had never been found. The tests were wrong. The detectives got confused; those ashes belonged to some other boys. The case remains open. I have that picture of him on my pinup board; I never took it down. He's still looking at me; over the years his smile has turned into a scowl. He's still not talking to me, unless he's talking at a volume that's deafening . . .

I know what you're thinking so let me be clear: I don't believe there's any link between the two boys, apart from a passing resemblance that incited the dream—the guy from the cemetery had a similarly fine bone structure. I'm not trying to suggest anything mystical. If the dead do return, regardless of the form, I doubt they would return whole; souls are way too intricate to enter unbroken into one body. I would wager souls multiply, divide, and subdivide, split like atoms into unsuspecting bodies, which would explain why we all feel so scattered, 'cos we're made up of the splintered bits of former human beings . . . Though if the kid isn't dead and somehow showed up at my door, naturally I would *make every attempt to restore what is his, as far as this is possible* . . .

The most troubling aspect of that encounter with the guy was my own reaction. I haven't been back to Holy Cross since then. I decided it wasn't in my interests. Not only had I failed to understand the dead, but I was getting too comfortable around them. The living have never put me at such ease. These days, I leave the house only when necessary.

As long as you lay low, stay quiet, don't let *D___h* hear you, *It* might just . . . glaze over you, go off in search of all the other names.

Of course you're free to go to the cemetery yourself during visiting hours. Maybe you could convince me to meet you, we could retrace our steps, I'd show you the message the guy carved in his unintelligible scrawl; it's actually on the bench where I always sat, by the grave of the Tin Man. He made me promise not to tell anyone what he wrote, and I plan to keep that promise, but you could try and decipher it. Maybe I would even go through with staying there all night. We could hide out in that concrete void until they lock the gates. My mind could be changed if you made the right offer.

Until then, I'll avert my gaze. At work, I make a concerted effort not to look at Holy Cross. Like it's not even there. Three hundred acres of nothing. *Alistair*, I tell myself, *don't look at it; look away.*

Though sometimes, on the bus, I do catch myself gazing at the hearses on the way to the cemetery. I know I've been rambling, giddy in your . . . presence, but that's what I wanted to tell you about.

The hearses slow the bus's progress down, but that's okay. The hearse driver is going to work, just like me. The corpse is going to work too. The hearses are shiny and black and luxurious, like limousines.

Driving a hearse is probably not that dissimilar to driving a limo. Both hearse drivers and chauffeurs are required to wear black—black suits and black gloves and black caps—and the relationship between the hearse driver and his client is formal and stiff, similar to the relationship between a chauffeur and his rich client.

Yet in some situations, the rapport between the hearse driver and his corpse must be easy-going, like the rapport established between a cab driver and his paying customer. The driver probably asks the corpse lots of questions, such as, *how did you die? Did it feel weird being sucked through the hole in the world?* And, *so what's it like exactly, tell me, how dark is Death?*

I've observed that hearses provide different levels of visibility: some hearses have tinted windows and black paneling on the sides, so you can't see inside at all. These models remind me of those windowless panel vans that were around in the 1970s. *Shaggin' Wagons*, we called them: vehicles in which teenagers got drunk and stoned and had sex.

Shaggin' Wagons were distinct from hearses, in that they were typically spray-painted with lurid designs, customized to showcase the driver's personality. Hearses tend to be fairly plain, as if the designers of these automobiles are intimating that death destroys the singular, the idiosyncratic, a corpse has no personality, or that death is ornate enough and there's no need for embellishment.

Distinctions aside, and contradicting the lack of visibility, just like when you spied someone climbing into a Shaggin' Wagon—you knew why they were entering the vehicle—when you spot someone being carried into a hearse, you know the exact reason they're going in. So perhaps the relationship between the driver and the corpse is as carnal and amorous as the charge between two lovers.

Other hearses have windows with clear glass, so you can see the licorice-black upholstery, but the windows in the rear of the vehicle always have curtains. The curtains are drawn to varying extents.

Some are drawn partly and some are drawn fully, obliterating the view. I'm uncertain of the degrees of symbolism—fully drawn, half-drawn, quarter-drawn—but I know I respond most strongly to those hearses where the curtains are almost drawn completely, open just a few inches.

That glimpse of the coffin, the sun illuminating a fraction of its surface—in the sun's rays, a coffin built from polished red wood glows like glace cherries in a liquor-drunk fruitcake—makes me want to know what's going on inside the hearse even more. Sometimes I look so hard trying to see, I get a crook in my neck!

At times I fantasize about biting the bullet, getting my license and becoming a hearse driver. This might satisfy my curiosity. But what's the point in learning how to drive if you can't drive yourself from the morgue to the cemetery? Anyway, I'll get to see a hearse firsthand, close up, one day.

On that day, my corpse, my last possession—life is just a long list of possessions: my cradle, my name, my grave, yet does my corpse truly belong to me?—*the* corpse bearing my name, the corpse that is imitating me and is therefore an impostor, will be placed in a coffin of a style that is yet to be determined and loaded gently or clumsily into the back of a hearse. The hearse will be shiny like the ones I've seen; no, this hearse will be shinier, so shiny I would be able to discern my own reflection in its glossy blackness, if I could still see; no, not just me, everyone will be able to discern their own reflection in the exterior of my hearse, yes, mine.

I imagine this last ride will be like those long drives we went on as kids with our parents. I had to sit in the back of my dad's station wagon, with his gardening tools that were not incompatible with the tools of a gravedigger, his shovel scraping against me, resting my head on a big bag of fertilizer, a hint of the fertilizer I will become, an indication of the stink from inside my coffin that will creep into the hearse's deodorized interior. Time inside a hearse will have that dragged-out quality it had in childhood; there'll be the same distorted sense of space and time converging into something . . . endless.

Just like a kid, my corpse will be excited, overly so, but will soon grow bored. Curtains or no curtains, I won't have the option of looking out the hearse's back window. Unable to lie there quietly, my corpse will fidget in its coffin and call out to the hearse driver, who, dressed in his skintight uniform, will be unable to hear me:

Are we there yet? Are we there?

A Note on Sources

Like the narrator of this book, I relied on various pockets of the Internet to acquire information about death and about the dead. I avoided academic and "expert" sources as much as possible; I wanted my information to be coming from sites, mainstream or obscure, that anyone curious about death could access. However, this is a work of fiction: while some of the facts have been reported accurately, many others, in particular pertaining to the lives and deaths of the characters, have been freely distorted.

I am indebted to the following sources: Carmelo Amalfi's "End in Sight" on *Fremantle Herald Interactive*, 2013; Susan Atkins's "Story of Two Nights of Murder" on Cielodrive.com, 1969; Vincent Bugliosi and Curt Gentry's *Helter Skelter*, 1974; Katherine Butler's "Five Weird Things That Happen after You Die" on Mother Nature Network, 2013; "California Screaming: An Interview with Brendan Mullen" on *3 AM Magazine*, 2002; Chris Campion's "Darby Crash: Saint Anger" on Dazed, 2014; Vincee Chavarria's "Venice: Community Mourns Murdered Mother to Be" on the Argonaut, 2009; CrimeNet's entry on Catherine and David Birnie in their "Serial Killer Crime Index," 2012; "Death Valley National Park Geology" on Oh, Ranger!, n.d.; "Devils in the Desert: Charles Manson's Preferred Hellmouth," as posted by Jeff on weirdthings.com, 2009; various dictionaries, including *The American Heritage Dictionary of the English Language*, Dictionary.com, the *Merriam-Webster Dictionary*, the *Online Etymology Dictionary*, the *Oxford Dictionary of Current English*, and *Wordnik*; Dignity Memorial's "Glossary of Funeral Terms," n.d.; DimensionsInfo's "Grave Dimensions," 2012; Robert Draper's "Called to the Holy Mountain: The

Monks of Mount Athos," which appeared in *National Geographic Magazine* in 2009; Dying Scene's "10 Things You Probably Didn't Know about Darby Crash," 2014, posted by Cyco Loco; Egyphile's lyrical response to the question "What does a dead body smell like?" on Yahoo!Answers, 2008; Robert Faturechi and Richard Winton's "Suspect in Venice Slaying Had Been Held by Culver City Police Days Earlier" in the *Los Angeles Times*, 2010; Robert Faturechi and Andrew Blankstein's "Venice Landlord Describes Attack on Victim of Rape-Slaying" in the *Los Angeles Times*, 2009; Funeralplan.com's "Burial Vaults and Grave Liners—A Consumer's Guide," 2001–3; Adam Gorightly's "Charles Manson and the Underground Stream" on The Konformist, 2001; my question "How long does it take for a human body to decompose," answered precisely on FunTrivia, 2008, Quora, 2016, and Yahoo!Answers, 2007; Esther Ingliss-Arkell's "10 Bodily Functions That Continue after Death" on io9, 2011; information on graves at Holy Cross Cemetery on Find a Grave Memorial, n.d., and Seeing Stars, 2016; the "HolyCrossMortuary" pages on Catholicmortuaries.com; the IMDb biography for Bela Lugosi; Victoria Laurie's "When Erin Chose to Die" in the *Australian*, 2008; the Lazarus Data Recovery site; Memorialpages' "Facts: What Happens to a Body after Death," 2005; the *Murderpedia* entry for David John Birnie, n.d., especially Paul B. Kidd's "The Birnies: Australia's House of Horrors," where I found Bill Powers's account of the Birnies' trial for the Perth *Daily News*; "Ocular Melanoma" on the "USC Roski Eye Institute" page on Keckmedicine, US National Library of Medicine, We Are Macmillan Cancer Support; the *Oxfordshire Bereavement Guide*; Psychobabble's "20 Things You May Not Have Known about Bela Lugosi," 2010; Krista Schwimmer's "Keeping Vigil for Eun Kang" in the *Free Venice Beachhead*, 2011; John Soennichsen's *Live! From Death Valley: Dispatches from America's Low Point*, 2005; Bill Stern's "Painting the Town" in the *Los Angeles Times*, 1997; Franny Syufy's "Guide to Cat's Eyes" on about.com, 2016; TodayIFoundOut.com's "The Difference between a Coffin and a Casket," 2011; David Urbinato's "London's Historic 'Pea-Soupers'" in the EPA journal, 1994; US Funerals Online's "Guide to Choosing a Grave Marker or Headstone," 2016; Weird California's "Deep into the Valley of Death We Go," as posted on Weird U.S., n.d.; Elizabeth Wetsch's entry on David and Catherine Birnie on crimezzz. net, 1995–2005; "When a dead person is getting embalmed do they makes noises?" on Yahoo!Answers, 2010; "Why do babies cry at the time of birth?" answered thoroughly by posts on Quora, 2015; Sara Wolf's obituary for Jill Yip in the *LA Weekly*, 2001.

I am particularly grateful to the writers of the local news stories in the California Briefing section of the *Los Angeles Times*, as well as longer pieces in the California section—namely, Hector Becerra, Andrew Blankstein, Ari Bloomekatz, Martha Groves, Carl Hall, Victoria Kim, Seema Mehta, H. G. Rezas, Carla Rivera, Susannah Rosenblatt, Garrett Therolf, and Richard Winton.

Wikipedia was of course an invaluable source of information on everything death-related, from birth certificates to decomposition, from Philip Nitschke to Tetralogy of Fallot.

There were times I strayed from the Internet. *The World Book Encyclopedia*, 1957 edition, volumes C, D, F, I, and W, was essential to this book, along with *The 1972 World Book Yearbook*, covering the events of 1971.

The 1952 Revised Standard Version of the Holy Bible was a crucial reference point, as was the Shambhala classics edition of *The Tibetan Book of the Dead*.

Finally, I broke my rule once to refer to an academic source, namely Aino Passonen's magnificent article "The Hourglass Figure in Manzoni's I Promessi Sposi [The Betrothed]: Multiplicities in Flux, Spatial Form, and the Milanese Bread Riots of 1628," which appeared posthumously in *Mobs: An Interdisciplinary Inquiry*, edited by Nancy van Deusen and Leonard Michael Koff, 2011.

Acknowledgments

I'm deeply grateful to my mother, Beth McCartney, my colleague Kirsten Grimstad, and my friend Gleah Powers for our conversations about the dead. (Kirsten's eulogy for Aino Passonen, "The Passing of a Dear Friend," circulated through Antioch University e-mail in 2010, was also essential.)

Many thanks to my colleagues at Antioch University LA in the Undergraduate Studies Program and MFA Creative Writing Program, especially MFA chair Steve Heller.

I'm indebted to my agent, Terra Chalberg, for her astute aesthetic guidance and all-round support.

I'm profoundly grateful to everyone at the University of Wisconsin Press for their support and hard work on the book: Dennis Lloyd, director; Scott Mueller and Sheila McMahon for their incredible editing, as well as managing editor Adam Mehring; communications director Sheila Leary for her amazing work on promotions and marketing; marketing intern John Leinonen; sales and marketing manager Andrea Christofferson; acquisitions assistant Amber Rose; rights and permissions manager Anne McKenna; production assistant Patrick Flynn; and the designer of the book cover, Jeremy Parker.

A special thanks must go to executive editor Raphael Kadushin for believing in this book and his unequivocal support.

Thank you to Cezar Popescu, curator of the Costică Acsinte Archive, for providing the image for the front cover of this book. The photograph is one of thousands made by Costică Acsinte, a Romanian photographer, active during World War I and later. Discover more of his photographs and portraits at http://colectiacosticaacsinte.eu.

And eternal thanks, always, to my husband, Tim Miller, for believing in me, for supporting me emotionally during the difficult and long process of completing this book, and for his keen and insightful reading of this book through various drafts.

Alistair McCartney is the author of *The End of the World Book*, a finalist for the PEN USA Literary Award in Fiction and the Edmund White Award for Debut Fiction given by the Publishing Triangle. He teaches fiction in the MFA program at Antioch University Los Angeles and oversees the undergraduate creative writing concentration. Born in Australia, he lives in Venice, California.